HIDDEN GOLD

HIDDEN GOLD

STEVE FRAZEE

Thorndike Press • Chivers Press
Thorndike, Maine USA   Bath, England

This Large Print edition is published by Thorndike Press, USA and by Chivers Press, England.

Published in 1998 in the U.S. by arrangement with Golden West Literary Agency.

Published in 1998 in the U.K. by arrangement with Golden West Literary Agency.

U.S. Hardcover 0-7862-0766-3 (Western Series Edition)
U.K. Hardcover 0-7540-3347-3 (Chivers Large Print)
U.K. Softcover 0-7540-3348-1 (Camden Large Print)

Thorndike Large Print ® Western Series.

The text of this Large Print edition is unabridged.
Other aspects of the book may vary from the original edition.

Set in 16 pt. Plantin by Rick Gundberg.

Printed in the United States on permanent paper.

British Library Cataloguing in Publication Data available

Library of Congress Cataloging in Publication Data

Frazee, Steve, 1909–
    Hidden gold : a Western story / Steve Frazee.
        p.   cm.
    ISBN 0-7862-0766-3 (lg. print : hc : alk. paper)
    1. Large type books. I. Title.
    [PS3556.R358H53   1998]
    813'.54—dc21   98-5425

HIDDEN GOLD

Chapter One

Brock Sargent thought he had a general idea of the country, but, when he rode from the keyhole of Antoro Pass, his first look at Weston County was like a blow in the stomach. Through heat haze the land lay drab and savage six thousand feet below him, a great sheet of brown, wrinkled by cañons and studded with rock domes. From here it appeared to be the poorest place in the world to start a ranch. He hoped that Pat Volpondo had made sure there was room for cattle to move between the rocks.

He lit his pipe under a shield of square-tipped fingers while the cold wind of the pass pushed against his faded jumper. Everything he owned was with him. Everything he hoped to own was there, below him. He sat the saddle of his blue roan gelding as if time meant nothing; but he was late now by forty-eight hours. He might have been a drifting rider. The difference lay in dark, judging eyes and a grave, almost solemn, composure of facial muscles. For several minutes he studied the salient fea-

7

tures of the land below, and then he started down.

Two hours later he was welcomed to Weston County by the quiet stare of a pistol. The owner had been sitting on a rock, saddle high to a dun that was cropping bunch grass. Sargent saw him an instant before the man moved like a lizard, leaping from the rock, dragging the pistol from his chaps pocket.

The man's thin-skinned face was chapped into red scales by the sun. He was burly, with pale gray eyebrows that twisted upward in little straggles. It did not take him long to see what he wanted to know — Sargent's bedroll, the war bag, the absence of a gun belt. He dropped his pistol back into his pocket without buttoning the flap.

"Not many riders use Antoro," he said. Pale blue eyes weighed Sargent carefully.

Sargent left his hands on the saddle horn and let the weight of the situation bear upon the man below.

"Well, come on down," the fellow said.

The dun was branded Triangle Y. Anchor was the other spread in Weston County, Sargent knew. He went on down and sat there, boring away with silence. The blistered man did not like it. Neither had Sargent liked the twisting feeling inside him during the moments he had been under the man's authority.

"You looking for a job?" the fellow said.

"I'm looking for a place to settle on my own."

"North of the Sodas, huh?"

Sargent looked across the violent landscape. Weston was a gray mark near the lava plain, a flat expanse that ran to the pale Soda Mountains in the distance. "Here," Sargent said.

"Cattle?"

Sargent nodded.

"It's rocky here, brother."

"I've seen grass around every rock, and little aspen parks that I couldn't see from the pass."

"There's already a cow for every bite of grass."

"This is the place." The gravity of Sargent's face was unchanged.

"You wouldn't want to crowd things, would you?"

"No. I like to stand shoulder wide and let the other fellow stand the same way."

Some mockery lay in the pale eyes of the red-faced man. He did not turn his head when the sound of a trotting horse came from the rocks to the south. "Well, settler, if you figure to see the town first, you're headed right to cut the trail of a Triangle herd that went down yesterday."

"Thanks."

Sargent watched a rider weave toward them at a pace which showed the man did not mind knocking hide off an animal's legs. Another Triangle horse. They came small and wiry for this rocky work, Sargent thought.

The rider came up with urgency, stopped quickly. He braced one foot against a rock and began to roll a cigarette. He was a slender man with a clear olive skin and a careless, friendly look about him. Sargent thought his clothes were too good, too neat for a working rider.

"We got a settler here, Chuck," the burly man said. He made it sound like a nester.

"Is that a fact?" Chuck did not seem interested after one quick glance at Sargent. "Nothing at the head of Griffin Park, Whitey."

"Work the oak brush west of Theobold's old place. Comb it good. You know where to hold the stuff till I get there." Whitey gave his orders curtly.

"Sure." The slender man took his time with the cigarette. He removed his hat and then re-set it carefully on curly brown hair. Sargent noted there was not a rock mark on the legs of his mount.

"Get going, Chuck," Whitey said.

"I'm gone." Chuck whirled his horse so quickly its hindquarters bumped a rock. He used his body and his knees as reins to guide his mount at a lope through places so narrow that Sargent instinctively crowded his own knees tighter against Windy, the blue roan.

"How far this way does Triangle range run?" Sargent asked.

Whitey's voice was expressionless. "Wherever there's a bunch of grass."

According to what Pat Volpondo had said, this country directly under Antoro Pass was neither Triangle nor Anchor range. Neither was it V Bar S — not yet. Sargent said: "Be seeing you."

He looked back once. Whitey was watching him, standing with his head bunched into his shoulders. Settling where others were already established would naturally create little problems. Volpondo had sized up this country. He was here now. In a few days the two of them would have a fair line on what must be faced.

Chapter Two

The sun was over the high point when Sargent found Volpondo. Quarreling magpies led him on foot into a scrub oak thicket just off a trail chopped by cattle hoofs. The sight beside the ant hill sent Sargent's eyes deeper into their sockets and left only beard-stubbled skin showing around his mouth.

Volpondo was the only man he had ever called friend. They had grown up together on the same ranch. The only way Sargent knew Volpondo now was by a hand-tooled belt and a turquoise ring that was sinking into swelling flesh. The marks of stirrup iron on the instep and heel of a small boot told the story of a man who had gambled once too often with a dangerous horse. He must have been dragged at a gallop for miles.

Sargent broke a branch and tried to sweep away the ants. He knew how futile it was, but for a moment it was all he could do. Then he dropped the branch and got the tarpaulin from the bedroll. The ants swarmed up his wrists as he worked. His mind was numb.

There was a buckskin money belt, worn almost in two. It was packed with bank notes.

Back-tracking later, Sargent found wisps of sorrel hair on the stubs of broken branches. The horse had crashed downhill on an angling course, blasting its way through the scrub oak. Sargent went back for a half mile to where the horse had left the trail on a switchback, and there the sign was lost under cattle tracks.

A thrown shoe had cost Sargent two days on the way from Wyoming. Volpondo had left word in Alder that he had gone on to Weston and to meet him there. One day to cross the Emigrants. . . . This had happened yesterday before Triangle brought the herd down.

On his way back to the body, Sargent studied the rock-hemmed, dusty trail. The riders had stayed behind with catch dogs working the flanks of the herd.

Sargent roped Volpondo across the saddle. He stood for a few moments, looking at a wisp of sorrel hair. Pat had left Alder on a stallion of that color, a big, powerful hellbinder, the kind he always favored. Sargent dropped the hair and ground his bootheel against it.

The trail to Weston meant nothing now.

Sargent no longer studied the bunch grass or sized up the aspen thickets. The bright fall day had turned bleak, and Weston County was not a promise but just a name. The tarpaulin swayed, and the motion caused a staining of the saddle skirts. A dozen times Sargent stopped walking to brush ants from the gelding's flanks when the tired animal started pitching.

At sunset Sargent came to the edge of a piñon mesa above the bright mark of the Sweetwater River. Weston lay below him, gray, dead, except for bawling cattle where riders were loading at the chutes near a rust-red railroad station. Much closer, on a piñon slope directly below, a patch of plaid and black and faded blue and gray was gathered around an open grave. A voice was running softly. The words did not come to Sargent, but the meaning was there. He removed his hat. The soft voice stopped. Hats went up on heads. The colors broke apart as energy contained a moment at the grave scattered men and women toward horses and wagons.

Gray gingham stayed on, gesturing around a girl whose hair shone rich brown in the dying sun. Sargent saw her shake her head as a woman pointed toward the last waiting wagon. A little later she was standing alone, except for a man leaning on a shovel.

Sargent waited where he was, with his hat in his hands and Windy blowing at his shoulder, until the girl walked away. She went straight-backed, walking steadily, a small figure dressed in gray clothes that did not seem to fit. She left with no back-glancing, and that was as final as the grave.

The man with the shovel saw Sargent when he came from the piñons, but the fellow did not stop his work until Sargent was quite close. He was a lean, middle-aged man with the grayness of his clothing extending to his sweaty face. His eyes ran past Sargent to the tarpaulin.

"A day for burying," the gray man said without expression.

"I'd like to borrow your tools when you're finished."

The man looked at Sargent's boots. "You've walked a fair piece, friend. I'll do it. Preacher just left. Ask for Theobold at the Lava House."

"I thank you."

The man helped take the burden from Windy.

In spite of his burned and blistered feet, Sargent did not go up in the saddle. He was leading the blue roan away when the gray man said: "Morton's livery. Put him in the third stall on the left."

Weston had boomed, then dried like a broken branch. The living part was drawn together at the west end, away from buildings with dim interiors and open, dusty eyes. Sargent walked past three blocks of dead buildings before he came to Morton's livery stable. It had room for fifty horses. There were five inside. Behind the barn was a freight yard where high-wheelers were warping into ruin.

Volpondo had said there were two hundred people in Weston. Sargent did not see a dozen after he took care of Windy and went down the street. There were two women in a general store. In front of it two bearded prospectors loaded burros. Their clothing was marked with the pale color of the Soda Mountains, and in their eyes was the gleam that is either hope or madness.

Sargent passed The Crusher Saloon. Three men were playing cards in there. The sign of the Lava House was hanging by one frayed piece of small cable. Dirty windows made the interior dim. Two women with faces marked by the harshness of the country were sitting in lumpy leather chairs in the lobby. Their hands were in their laps. Their eyes were sharp but not expressive.

16

They had been to the funeral, Sargent guessed, and now they were waiting for their husbands to be done with business some place.

He touched his hat to them as he crossed a dirty floor to the desk. A small bell that he palmed made a futile sound against the decadence of the room. One of the women said: "You're wasting time, young man. Go take the outside stairs to the roof."

"I'm looking for the preacher."

"That's him. He runs this place."

The stairway was so dry rotted that Sargent risked weight only close to the cleats of the steps. He turned from a balcony that ran across the back of the hotel and followed a short flight of steps to the roof. A big man in black broadcloth was sitting in a leather-bottomed chair, looking beyond the railroad station to the Emigrant Mountains. He did not glance at Sargent.

"Mister Theobold?"

"Yes." Both the fact and the question seemed to annoy the man.

"You're the preacher?"

"I sometimes serve as such."

"There is a dead man at the graveyard."

"Oh?" Theobold looked at Sargent then for the first time. He was shining clean, carefully shaved. His sandy hair was closely

17

cut, lying like a thick tufted cap upon his wide head. The heavy bony structure of his face and a directness in his eyes marked him as a fighter, a man far apart from the decay upon which he sat, but there was a boredom in his whole expression when he said that single word.

"Will you come up?" Sargent asked.

"Yes. Are you ready now?"

Sargent glanced at the only building in town that could be the courthouse. "Will a half hour be all right?"

"Yes."

It was impossible that a man so neat and clean, obviously not sick, could be so listless, Sargent thought. Once more Sargent glanced in the direction of the courthouse, but this time no farther than across the street where a girl was hoeing in a garden beside a small house. She had changed her clothes, but it was the same girl he had seen at the grave.

"Alma Burent," Theobold said. "It was her father we buried while you stood watching from the piñons. You removed your hat, I noticed." Theobold smiled briefly at Sargent's level gaze. "Some people claim that my eyes are the only faculty I use." He looked towards the mountains again, settling a little lower in the chair. "Your dead man,

I presume, departed for less violent reasons than John Burent."

"A horse dragged him," Sargent said curtly.

"Unfortunate. Burent was murdered."

Unfortunate! A natural disliking of townsmen began to kindle anger in Sargent.

"You'll stay a night, at least?" Theobold asked.

"I might."

"Take the corner room, southwest, first floor. It's cooler sometimes. I think it was shoveled out last month. If you care to register, you'll find one under the desk." Theobold took a cigar from his pocket, still looking at the mountains. "A half hour then, Mister . . . ?"

"Sargent."

He went back down the rickety steps. The garden where Alma Burent was working was the only one Sargent had seen in Weston. The house was old and weather-battered, but the windows were clean. The yard was uncluttered.

As Sargent passed, the girl raised her head to brush her brow with a forearm. Her face was a small oval, finely drawn so that the largeness of her eyes was emphasized. He touched his hat. She nodded slightly, appraising him for an instant before she bent to her work again. She was trying to chase grief before a burst of energy, Sargent thought. He knew how she felt.

He passed a leaning fireplug, sad with rust. The valve was high, and there was sand in the threads of a dry mouth. Locust trees around the courthouse were dying for lack of water that ran in a ditch forty feet away. There had been a lawn once. Energy and planning had gone into the sandstone courthouse, but both had died just above unfinished openings for second-story windows, and there the roof had been born prematurely.

Lettering on an open door inside said **Sheriff**. The man with his feet on the sill of an open window gave the impression of wearing skin as loose as his dark clothes. The brim of his hat was too wide for his narrow face. His eyes were bloodshot with dark pockets under them.

He said: "Morse Tallman, sheriff of Weston County. I hope I can help you." He did not take his feet from the window sill.

"There's a man at the graveyard. I found him six, seven miles this side of Antoro Pass."

Tallman blinked. "What got him?"

"His horse dragged him." If the sheriff

20

did not take his feet from the window sill, Sargent was going to kick them loose in a moment. He had had about enough of Weston lassitude.

One at a time Tallman put his feet on the floor. He rose, a tall man so long in the waist that his vest was several inches short. "I'll take a look. I don't much fancy it. Who are you?"

"Brock Sargent."

Tallman took a gun belt from a peg and strapped it around him. "There used to be some Sargents in Emigrant County."

"A long time ago."

They crossed the scabby patches of the yard. The sun was gone, but the air was still stagnant with heat. Tallman walked with a long stride. When they passed the Burent house, the sheriff lifted his hat to the girl and said with forced cheerfulness: "A good crop this year, Alma?"

"The best yet." She glanced at Sargent.

When they were out of earshot, Tallman muttered: "We buried her father today." He looked with disgust at the crumbling town. "A hell of a place for a woman alone. Bad enough for a man."

"The railroad runs, doesn't it?"

Tallman's narrow face swung quickly. He

21

sorted questions in his mind. "You drifted in for the roundup, did you?"

"I had planned to settle here."

"Where?"

"The East Fork of the Sweetwater."

The sheriff nodded. "Theobold controls the country up that way. You might have been able to deal with him. You might have made a go of it, too. You're young, you look durable . . . and you're insulting enough."

Theobold came down his stairs, walking close to the ends of the steps as Sargent had done.

"We'll walk, Tracy," the sheriff said.

Theobold smiled. "I don't mind . . . if you don't lecture me on the benefits of exercise."

Their boots made little swishing sounds as they walked up the middle of the sandy street. There was not another living thing in sight.

"How many people here?" Sargent asked.

"Fewer than there was last year," Theobold said. "Perhaps a hundred. How many of them vote, Morse?"

The sheriff grunted.

"Where are they?" Sargent asked.

"Voters and all, they're getting rich digging gold between here and the lava."

Theobold smiled.

The grave was dug, not deep but enough. "Hot work," Tallman said to the gray man. "You met Sargent, did you, Morton?"

"We met." Morton leaned on his shovel.

The obscene bumbling of flies sickened Sargent as he unwrapped the tarp. Tallman took a quick breath, his narrow features draining to a leaden color. Something quick and hard flashed in his bloodshot eyes. "God, yes!" he muttered. "He was dragged." His throat muscles jerked.

They buried Pat Volpondo. Theobold's words ran soft and simply. They rolled back the years to distant memories of Sargent's boyhood with the dead man — that made it worse, for the loss was not today's but of a lifetime.

". . . let him see the morning on a new and beautiful range. We ask these things in His name. Amen."

Theobold turned away, looking toward the Emigrants. He was not a bored man then, Sargent thought, and he had been sincere. The heavy bones of his face looked blunt in the dying light.

Morton pointed toward town with his eyes. Theobold did not walk with the sheriff and Sargent when they left. He went slowly up the hill. Tallman studied Sargent for a long time before he spoke.

"You knew him?"

"I did," Sargent said.

"Pat Volpondo."

"How did you know?"

"The little feet. The turquoise ring. He was proud of that belt, Sargent. A friend sent it to him from Wyoming."

"Me," Sargent said.

They came to the edge of the town.

"Who are you?" Tallman asked.

"I told you."

"You gave me a name."

"It's mine. What's on your mind, Tallman?"

"Come down to my office in about an hour."

"What's the matter with now?" Sargent asked.

"The county clerk will be cooking his supper in his office. His ears are too big."

"You can close your door."

"In about an hour, Sargent," Tallman said.

When they approached the livery stable, the sheriff veered toward it — *to check the brand on my horse,* Sargent thought. He went on alone toward The Crusher. He was on the outside of something that was going on in Weston. If it had anything to do with Pat Volpondo, he would be on the inside before he finished. He looked at the brands on two horses before the saloon, one Anchor, one Triangle Y.

The Crusher was large. It had the feel of a place where hell had roared once. Now there were two lights, one at the end of a long bar where two cowboys were drinking, another above a poker table where five men sat. A little man left the game and went behind the bar when Sargent stepped near the two cowboys.

"A bottle," Sargent said to him.

"We got one kind." The little bartender's voice was a hoarse whisper. A bottle and a glass thumped the bar. The man went back to his game.

Sargent sat down at a table. One drink ran slow warmth through his body. He felt the weariness of his legs. The poker players were railroaders, he decided. The two at the bar were the ones he wanted to talk to. One was a square-rigged man with a barrel chest and tremendous shoulders. The Triangle horse outside would go a strong twelve hundred pounds. This big man with the broken nose and blocky features must be the owner. The second man was quick-eyed, lean, with a week's growth of black whiskers against flat cheeks. When he glanced casually at Sargent, the latter touched the bottle and nodded.

"Free roll, Pete," the lean man said. "Bring the glasses before he changes his mind."

They came to the table, the man called Pete with a rolling walk that shook the floor. Twisted wire on the chair legs twanged as he sat down and introduced himself and his companion. Pete Weston and Clum Brand.

"Been loading cattle all afternoon," Weston said. "We'll likely work half the night because the stinking railroad didn't get the cars here they promised." He let the words roll, and then he followed up by staring at the men playing poker. One player, a squat, beetle-browed man, returned the challenge, unimpressed.

"I followed your sign in from below Antoro Pass," Sargent said. "You picked up the herd yesterday?"

"Yep." Brand poured himself a drink, and then another.

"I thought you were Anchor," Sargent said.

Brand nodded. "Good guess. We help each other out, up there in the rocks."

"I found a dead man near that trail today," Sargent said. "His horse came down before the cattle did."

Weston's face came around with a jerk. He had been looking toward the poker table. "The hell you say?" He was amiable enough, interested.

Brand's eyes were hooded at the corners. "Who was it?"

Sargent shook his head. "His horse dragged him . . . a long ways."

Weston and Brand looked at each other. "Chuck Ozanne!" Brand said. "I knew he was going to get it, the way he rides that country."

"I met a Chuck and a Whitey today," Sargent said. "Chuck was a good-looking, curly-haired fellow, alive."

Weston leaned back in his chair. "I'm glad to hear it wasn't Chuck." He sized up Sargent closely.

Pete Weston might be a slow-thinking man, Sargent decided, but he was not stupid, and he was setting himself now for certain conclusions that Sargent's line of questioning had indicated.

"The horse had used the trail, for a ways," Sargent said. "The oak brush where I found him was swarming with crows and magpies."

The poker game was at a standstill. Sargent's statements left a flatness, a waiting in the room. Anger began to gather in bright lumps on Weston's face.

"Say on," he invited. "You wonder why we didn't see the sign. Say it, mister."

"I wonder why."

"Don't bust your rope, Pete," Brand said quickly. He looked at Sargent. "We ride behind up there. We use catch dogs. We raise a pile of dust."

"That's what I thought," Sargent said evenly. "I wanted to hear it said."

Weston was not satisfied. He kept mulling things over, staring.

Brand tried to talk the tightness away. "Just where at was this place?" he asked.

Sargent described the country close to the oak thicket.

"We couldn't see our saddle horns when we went past there," Brand said. "That ought to answer anything you're thinking."

"I made it blunt," Sargent said. "I take no offense at blunt answers."

Weston was still staring past his broken nose. It was a strongly rooted nose, and it must have taken a fearful blow to smash it. "It was pretty blunt, all right." Weston rubbed his lips together. "I didn't like it."

"Slow down, Pete." Brand was nervous. "The man didn't try to ride you. He talked straight out."

Sargent did not want trouble. Weston was leaving the door wide open for it, trying to work it in. They watched each other, Sargent leaning back in his chair, his face grave, steady. It was Weston who veered away finally. He was not afraid, Sargent observed, not in the least afraid. It would not take much to tip him into action.

Brand made the break. "Thanks for the drinks." He rose. "Pete, we'd better get back to the herd before Gin falls asleep."

"No rush," Weston said. He took another drink, eyeing Sargent over the glass, and then went out with Brand. His weight shook the floor.

"You fancy yourself as a fist fighter, cowboy?" The little bartender looked at Sargent.

"Not especially."

"Well, then, you might have overmatched yourself something awful. Give me two cards, Gipp."

"I've seen Pete Weston whipped, Boley," one of the players said. "Up at Turret once."

"I ain't never," Boley said in his hoarse whisper. He threw his hand away. "I ain't never."

Sargent asked: "Is he one of the Weston County Westons?"

"The last," Boley answered. "The last."

A man with a brakeman's club beside his chair riffled his chips. "I hear he's going to marry old Fletcher Hitchcock's daughter."

"She ain't Hitchcock's daughter," Boley said. "And Pete ain't quite that dumb, even though he still was sitting in the fifth grade when he weighed two hundred pounds."

Sargent waited, drinking little, gnawed by a restlessness that did not show on his face. A rheumy-eyed man with a stained white mustache hurried in and took a seat at the poker table.

The black-browed railroader named Gipp said: "You cooked supper in a hurry, Hadley. What's Tallman found out since noon?"

Hadley put on glasses and counted the stack Boley shoved toward him. "You don't find out things sitting with your feet on a window sill."

"Tallman was out on the lava all morning," someone said.

"So was everyone else," Boley said. "So was. . . ."

The poker players laughed.

Sargent reasoned Hadley must be the county clerk. Tallman had no excuse for further stalling. Sargent had paid for the drinks and was heading toward the doors when he heard someone at the poker table ask: "Who's he, anyway?"

Once outside a tall form came out of the semi-darkness and approached Sargent. It was Morton. He stopped at the edge of the walk and said solemnly: "This was hanging about half way out of your saddlebags." He gave Volpondo's money belt to Sargent.

"Thanks."

"Did that man today use stirrups built too small for his feet?"

"I never knew him to."

"That boot was awful small to hang up on an average stirrup, Sargent." Morton cleared his throat. His face was a long, indistinct blob. "There was what you could call a rope burn on his left ankle. I looked after you were gone."

"I didn't notice."

"It is something to think about." Morton turned away, a gray man fading into the gloom of a deserted street.

Chapter Three

Sargent and Tallman reached the court-house almost at the same time, Tallman coming across the baked yard from the direction of the railroad station. The sheriff lit a brass lamp and sat down with his feet on the window sill. With his hat off, his black hair rising in a bristly sweep, he was a younger man than he had appeared earlier.

"Sit down," he said. "You're Brock Sargent, they say in Alder. Is that all you are?"

"That's all."

"All right." Tallman fanned at gnats swarming in the open window. "You didn't stop in Alder long, they say."

"Just long enough to find out Volpondo had ridden out two days earlier than I expected. I was late two days."

"You hadn't seen him much in the last four years, huh?"

"No."

"He was here three years ago. He talked about a Sargent in Wyoming. The two of you were going to have a ranch some day.

Volpondo asked a lot of questions about the East Fork country when he was here." Tallman nodded. "I guess you're the right man. I had to use the telegraph to make sure."

The heat of a dead day seemed to be gathered in the office. Beams creaked somewhere in the huge building.

Tallman rubbed his eyes. "Last Monday night, Wayne Hitchcock . . . a Western Express messenger . . . came in with a Smuggler Mine's payroll, a hundred and nine thousand dollars in gold. It should have been dumped off at Turret. It wasn't, because the Western agent there had caught a stray bullet from a gun fight and was in no shape to receive it. The guard unloaded at Turret. You know how those train guards are . . . Western grabs a teamster or a platform man and says . . . 'You're guard today. Check out a shotgun.' The guard said to hell with it. He was supposed to make the run to Turret, and that was it. He unloaded.

"Hitchcock wired back to the Western Division superintendent at Alder. The super said to bring the safe on here and unload it on John Burent, the Weston agent. Burent had a wire, too, to hold the safe overnight and send it back on the next day's train. By that time Western would have a relief agent in Turret to take it. All clear, so far?"

Sargent nodded.

"The safe is an iron box. You've seen them. It opens with a key. Gold and all, it weighed around seven hundred pounds. Hitchcock and Burent dumped it out of the express car here into Burent's wagon. It's three blocks from the station to the office. About half way four men rode out of the dark, no hurry, clubbed Burent and Hitchcock and took the safe."

"Seven hundred pounds?"

Tallman nodded wearily. "I was sitting at this window. I never heard a sound. It was about twenty minutes later that Joe Gipp and his fireman stumbled over Hitchcock and Burent. The team had gone right on up to the back of the Western office and stopped by the platform. Burent and Hitchcock were still laying in the street. The key to the safe was still in a sealed envelope in Burent's pouch. Burent lived until yesterday, but he never regained consciousness. They almost tore the top of Hitchcock's head off with a gun butt . . . I'd say it was . . . but he came to in about an hour."

The sheriff gave Sargent a long, questioning look.

"You didn't know that Pat Volpondo was

Western's crack agent for the mountain division?"

"Pat?"

"The really big deals, Sargent. The rest of the time he broke horses at Trinchera ranch."

"I never knew it."

Tallman blinked. "Western found it handy that way. Three years ago I went into the Sodas with Volpondo after three men that had dynamited an express car at Costilla Pass. We brought them back. That's how I knew Volpondo."

Sargent lit his pipe. It did not taste right. He put it back in his pocket.

"Volpondo had already quit Western," the sheriff continued. "He'd told 'em a month before all this that he was done, that he was going to settle down over here. They tried to talk him into investigating this job, and he wouldn't take it." Tallman shook his head slowly. "But someone who knew who he was thought he had taken the job. Pat Volpondo never let his foot get hung up in a stirrup, Sargent. What do you think?"

"I'm not sure. Pat was hell for cinch-binders."

Some of the heat began to creak out of the building as they sat, looking at each other. The dark streets of Weston were quiet.

"He *rode* his horses, Sargent. When I went into the Sodas with him, he was on a stallion that I wouldn't have tried to fork when I was sixteen." The sheriff bunched the muscles of one cheek and spat through the window. "Did Morton tell you about the rope burn? He said he was going to."

"He told me."

Tallman looked at the money belt Sargent had dropped on the desk. "That his?"

"Uhn-huh."

The money was in large notes. Tallman counted it carefully. "Four thousand dollars."

A life's work, a life's hope — Sargent had almost that much in a belt himself. It did not mean anything now. He kept seeing Volpondo's face when they were kids. He heard Theobold's soft words on the hill after sunset.

"I didn't have any doubts," Sargent said slowly. "But I had to know. I backtracked. Maybe not far enough. Then the money in the belt. . . ."

"Four thousand against a hundred thousand?" Tallman smiled thinly. "It looked good, didn't it?"

"You're mighty sure, Tallman."

"Without the facts I'm still mighty sure."

Sargent studied the sheriff. "Who all knew Pat was an agent for Western?"

"Hanawalt, the division superintendent, old Pegram, the Western owner, and me. I took it sort of prideful that I was the only sheriff in the whole division who knew." Tallman stared out at the quiet darkness. "Somebody else knew, though. That's a cinch."

"When he came here three years ago after those . . . ?"

"He came at night. We rode out at night, and, when we came back from the Sodas with one live man and the swag, Volpondo faded from the picture. I put the man and the money on the train the next day and went over to Alder. I got the credit for the job."

"All right, suppose somebody did kill Pat, like you figure. Why? These four men the other night got away with the safe, busted it open, took the gold. . . ."

"No, Sargent. They're not in the clear yet." The sheriff frowned. "It's got to be that way. We never found the safe. They must have buried it, or something." Tallman's face said that he was once more treading old ground that puzzled him. "It's either that, or the men are local people. They had to stop Volpondo. He did about ten tough jobs for Western, Sargent. He never muffed one."

"You pushed the four so hard they had to ditch the safe?" Sargent asked.

Red came up in Tallman's long face. "Pushed, hell! We went the wrong way, toward the Emigrants. Who'd figure four men with a heavy safe would head straight out toward an open lava plain? But that's exactly what they did, after a little circle that made us think they were headed the other way."

"How'd they handle that weight?"

"A rack of four wagon tongues, not too heavy. I figure the cross-pieces rested on their saddles."

"Sounds impossible."

"They did it," Tallman said. "I found where they dropped the safe once, crossing a steep gully near the river. They had an awful time loading it again. They went to the lava. They burned the rack, most of it. Then they went four ways." He gave Sargent time to think it over.

"Then the safe is between here and the lava?"

"It must be. That's why everybody in Weston is out digging. I got deputies there. There's Western agents, too. Five thousand reward for the safe." The sheriff regarded

Sargent intently. "It ain't there." Tallman looked confused. "I said it must be, but I still think it ain't."

"Why?"

"I can trail. When we got back at daylight from our goose chase toward the Emigrants, I finally got on the right track. Those four men went as fast as they could, and the sign said they never stopped but that one time they dropped the safe."

Sargent said: "Something doesn't fit."

"Yeah."

"Why did they tackle all that weight when the key was on Burent?"

"Maybe they didn't know that. It ain't hard to open one of those safes. A husky kid, a strong bar, that's all."

"The bunch of men looking for that gold right now are a bigger threat than Pat would have been. I can't see. . . . "

"I can. Volpondo wouldn't have wasted five minutes looking for the safe. He would have been after men, and, when he went after men, there was a payoff. They killed him."

Bitterness was coiling in Sargent. "You're sure the safe came off the train?"

"Two brakemen saw it dumped into the wagon. Billy Williams, the telegraph operator, saw it and so did the express messenger who relieves Hitchcock here, Jack Zellers." Tallman added what he did not seem to consider important. "Tracy Theobold saw it from his roof, three blocks away."

"But nobody saw the four men?"

"Nobody. They come up behind the wagon, riding slow. Hitchcock and Burent took them for some of the cowboys, holding a herd near the chutes."

"Who was in that bunch . . . at the chutes?"

"It was a mixed herd. Whitey Fallon, the Triangle foreman, was there with Clum Brand and Gin Carstairs. Gin runs the Anchor for Tug Marshall. Clum and Whitey was holding the herd. Gin was asleep. They hadn't seen anything unusual. Whitey went with us when we headed for the mountains."

Faint and mournful, a train whistle rode the night. Coyotes at the edge of town laughed and yapped. Dogs began to bay defiance.

Sargent stood at the window. "You think, then, that the gold is still in the box?"

"If it wasn't, why would they hide the safe?"

"That the same train coming in now?"

"Uhn-huh. It'll be here in about fifteen minutes."

Sargent turned away from the window,

brushing at gnats. He sat down on a corner of the desk. "This shooting at Turret that crippled the Western agent there . . . that fitted right into things, didn't it?"

"Right nice," Tallman agreed. "Before I even knew about it, Western had wired the marshal up there to hold the two men. One was dead, the one that accidentally shot the agent. The marshal had already chased the other one."

"Anyone from this end of the county?"

"Drifting toughs, according to the Turret marshal. They'd been in trouble before."

"It still fits fine," Sargent said.

"Uhn-huh."

After a few moments Sargent said: "Somebody knew for sure that safe was coming off the train here?"

"Not too hard to figure. Twice before, for different reasons, Smuggler payrolls were taken right on through Turret and then held here before going back. It made a sort of pattern to follow, I suppose."

"This Billy Williams, the telegrapher here . . . ?"

"Honest as the day is long. He wouldn't give a man the time if he thought it wasn't official business."

"Did Burent talk too much?"

"Close-mouthed as all get out."

41

"Who is the express agent here now?" Sargent asked.

"Alma Burent is handling things."

The train whistle came again, louder. Sargent walked to the doorway.

"I'll give you a receipt for the money, Sargent."

"No need." Ten years of peeling broncos at the Trinchera. Ten years of going without things to save money. Pat Volpondo had never had it easy, and his being a Mexican had made it even tougher for him at times. A receipt for money, a receipt for a dead dream.

Tallman walked across the room. "I'd like to see you settle here, Sargent, but I guess you don't think much of the country now."

At the moment Sargent hated everything about it. "I'll be seeing you, Tallman," he said. He walked into a night that seemed as hot as the day had been.

Chapter Four

A low-slung mountain Mikado engine ground past Sargent as he walked toward the freight platform at the station. Three passenger coaches passed, their occupants peering through the grimy windows with dim interest. Two men came down the steps of a coach and started toward the station. A brakeman called: "No lunch room, boys."

"What kind of dump is this?"

The brakeman laughed. "Weston."

Alma Burent was standing on the freight platform. Behind her, on the street side, a wagon was backed against the planks. Sargent started to speak but didn't. The express car door slid open. Quick light on the girl's face caught an expression of grief and stark loneliness; then she raised her chin and composed her features.

"Hello, Alma." The messenger who spoke from the doorway was a tall, pale man with hair clipped nakedly to his skull. The angry pocks of surgical stitches ran beside a long-healing scar on his head. "The telegrapher in Turret told us. I'm sorry, Alma."

"Thank you." She left no further opening for sympathy. "Anything for Weston?"

The messenger shook his head, glancing at Sargent. He put on a wide-brimmed hat gingerly. He waited in the doorway with a bag beside him.

"Hitchcock?" Sargent asked.

The messenger nodded.

"I'd like to talk to you."

"You guys are thicker than fleas these days."

"I'm not from the company," Sargent said. "But I want to talk to you."

Hitchcock said: "Can we use the office, Alma?"

Her glance at Sargent was not friendly. "Of course."

Hitchcock removed his hat carefully. They waited until one of the men Sargent had seen in the poker game came hurrying down the platform with a bag in his hand. "Well! You didn't take much time off, Hitchcock," he said.

"Who does, with this outfit?"

"How's the bean?"

"Sore," Hitchcock said. "One of these days, Zellers, you're going to stay one hand too long and miss the train."

The relief messenger laughed. "I won ten

44

bucks on that last hand! For twice that much you can have the train."

Sargent rode behind the seat of the wagon, with Alma driving and Hitchcock on the seat beside her. *If the night of the robbery had been as dark as this one,* Sargent thought, *it was no wonder the four men had not been seen.* Alma stopped the team where a lamp in a small office not far from the Lava House showed the galloping white horse window sign of Western Express.

"It's unlocked," she said.

Hitchcock reached for the lines. "Let me put the team away."

"I got it out myself," the girl said.

Hitchcock limped across the sidewalk ahead of Sargent. The office was clean, orderly. It had the sterile look of "no business here." Hitchcock sat down stiffly. In the full light he was a young man, sharp-featured, with wide-set blue eyes. "You're not from the company, then?" he asked.

Sargent shook his head. "Did you ever hear of Pat Volpondo?"

"Sure. The Mexican bronc' topper at the Trinchera ranch, near Alder. I live in Alder . . . half the time."

"He's dead."

Hitchcock blinked. His pale face held a puzzled look.

45

"Volpondo was a special agent for Western Express."

Lines running from the corners of Hitchcock's bold nose deepened as he tightened his lips and shook his head. "You must be thinking of somebody else. This Volpondo I knew of breaks horses."

"Uhn-huh. What makes you think he didn't work for Western, too?"

Hitchcock considered. "I guess it is possible, but Pat's a Mex, a ranch hand. . . ."

"He was my friend."

"I didn't mean. . . ."

"It's all right," Sargent said. "How many special agents do you know?"

Hitchcock grinned. Even then his face was tired. "I see your point. I do know two of our special agents. So this Mex . . . Volpondo . . . was another one, huh?"

Sargent looked around the barren office. "How can Weston keep this place going?"

"It can't. The company has been losing money on the office for about a year, but Burent and the Western big wheel, old Ike Pegram, used to freight together. Burent didn't want to move from here, so Pegram just sort of pensioned him off by letting the office stay open."

Sargent wondered, although it was none of his business, what would happen to Alma

Burent now. "Tallman tells me that nobody saw those four men last Monday night."

"They were walking their horses. They came alongside us like that. We thought they were some of the boys from the herd at the chutes. They were on top of us before I saw a mask. I got the button of my holster unsnapped. Burent got the shotgun up from across his knees." Hitchcock's naked head made a tremendous, wagging shadow on the wall. "That was before the roof came down."

He's still shaky from that ripped head, Sargent thought. "You're sure there was four?"

"I thought five or six, but the tracks showed four."

"Did they say anything?" Sargent asked.

"Just that whistling."

"Any markings on the horses?"

"I was looking at a mask and digging at my holster. As far as I know, the horses were any color."

Sargent nodded gloomily. He was going over old ground, he knew, but he wanted his answers first hand. "Except by telegraph, how could anyone here know that the safe was on the train?"

Hitchcock shook his head.

"As far as you know, the telegrapher and

Burent were the only ones who could have known?"

"Yeah," Hitchcock said.

"Alma?"

The messenger's eyes grew quick and light. "Special agent or not, take it easy, mister. Alma was with a sick woman here in town all day, right up until after the robbery."

"Could a horse beat the train from Turret to here?"

Hitchcock was no longer cooperative. "I don't know."

"Relays?"

"Maybe. I couldn't say."

Alma came in quietly. Both men rose, Hitchcock lurching a little before he steadied himself. His eyes were bitter when he saw that Sargent had observed.

The messenger said good night to the girl and went out. Sargent started to follow.

"Mister Sargent."

She was not what he would have called a pretty girl, but there was a cleanness and straightness in her eyes that made up for that. She did not dislike him, he observed. She hated his guts.

"You are a Western special agent, aren't you?"

He shook his head. "Not even the law. I had a friend who may have been killed because of this mess."

"I had a father killed because of it."

Sargent stood there uneasily, fingering his hat, not understanding what was driving her.

She said: "So now you're taking the law into your own hands."

"If things run that way, Miss Burent."

"All you want is vengeance."

Sargent moved his right hand impatiently. "Call it that, if you want to."

"What do you call it?"

She was asking questions that needed no answers. She was upset, illogical, under great strain, and yet she seemed to be thinking clearly on some basis of her own. Sargent edged toward the door.

She asked again: "What do you call it, Mister Sargent?"

"Something I *have* to do . . . if it turns out that way."

"What way?"

He opened his mouth, then closed it. "Good night."

Outside, he looked back to see her sitting on the edge of the desk, small, tense, her shoulders starting to sag. He felt better when three women passed him and turned into the office. That's what Alma Burent needed — woman talk.

He packed his pipe and lit it. The taste of the smoke told him he should have eaten hours before. He went around the corner past the Lava House. There was a dim light on the desk, like a dying candle on a coffin. Through the murky windows of The Crusher he saw the same poker game, a different crew of railroaders playing. Hadley, the county clerk, was there. Sheriff Tallman was watching. Sargent went on to the livery stable.

Ulysses Morton came down a stairway near the harness room after Sargent lit a lantern. He glanced at the bedroll on Sargent's shoulder. "Staying at the Lava House?"

"Yeah."

"You could've bunked here. You ain't ate, either. No place in Weston to eat. Come up. . . ."

"Thanks. I'm not hungry."

"Come over for breakfast, then."

"I will, thanks." Sargent put the bedroll down again. The feel of the blankets reminded him of where his tarp was. "Is Wayne Hitchcock, the express messenger, any relation to Fletcher Hitchcock?"

"Son," Morton said, "Old Fletch owns the Triangle."

Sargent kept waiting.

"They fell out about six years ago. That woman at the Triangle caused the trouble, I hear."

"What's wrong with Hitchcock's legs?"

"Six men stopped the train at Costilla Pass three years back. Wayne and the guard wouldn't open up the door of the express car. They started shooting back when the robbers did. The toughs dynamited the car. That killed the guard and smashed Hitchcock's knees."

"They get the robbers?" Sargent asked.

"A posse from Turret, led by that tough marshal, got three of them. Tallman got the other three and the loot, somewhere out in the Sodas a few days later."

"Just Tallman?"

"Sure. Don't make no mistake about him."

"Big job for one man."

"He did it, Sargent. Brought one back alive."

"What time was it when he came after his horse?"

"Late at night."

"When did he come back?"

"Night."

"Thanks, Morton. I'll be over for that breakfast."

Lantern light made hollows on Morton's gray face. "Do that," he said, and went back up the stairs.

Theobold was a big, solid figure near the bat wings of The Crusher when Sargent went down the street. Cigar smoke drifted out into air that was just beginning to lose the heat of day.

"A beautiful evening, Sargent."

"Uhn-huh."

"Weston may be dead, as some people say, but it's restful here. I think you'll find it that, at least."

Sargent thought of the newest grave up there on the dark piñon hillside. Some people would call that restful, too.

The corner room that Theobold had designated was musty with the smell of disuse. A match showed a lamp, its bowl a greasy mixture of spilled kerosene and dust. Sargent's feet left tracks across a brittle carpet. He wrenched up a window near the bed. Dust came down with a feathery touch on the back of his neck.

He dumped his bedroll on the bed, took his gun belt from inside, and hung it on a chair. He sat down in a platform rocker with brass-capped arms that were warm and gritty to the feel. Tomorrow night, if he were still here, he would throw his blankets under one of the warping ore wagons in Morton's yard.

The full weight of the day came down on him. In leaping sheets that started with his swinging down from Windy to walk into a scrub oak thicket he saw clearly what the day had done to him. Events had veered his life far away from the distant time when he had looked down on Weston County from a wet ledge at the keyhole of Antoro Pass.

Moths came in the window and flirted with the lamp. Only one side of the wick was burning now, streaking black inside the chimney, sending sooty odor into the room. Sargent leaned over and whisked his cupped hand above the chimney. The light died, sending up one last puff of greasy smoke.

Pat Volpondo had been a skinny little orphan with wide, scared brown eyes the day Sargent's uncle had brought him to the Double S near Alder. There were neighbors who said that Clay Sargent did not care whom he took in, including Mexican brats and stray dogs. All his life Pat had been forced to face that sort of attitude. He could have been a foreman on any ranch in the Alder country, except that he was a Mexican.

If it was unjust, it was nonetheless there. Pat and Sargent had learned to live with it. They went to one dance, when they were fifteen, and after that they never went again. Over here they would have had their own ranch. It would not have been mere ownership of land and cattle but proof that a man was as good as his acts, with the color of the skin not mattering.

The dream was dead now. All that mattered was to determine the manner of its going. It was Sargent's hope that any evidence he turned up tomorrow there on the trail below Antoro would show that Pat Volpondo had died solely because of a dangerous horse. Pat had never abused a horse. With his collar bone and one arm broken when he was thrown against a snubbing pole, he had laughed about the horse that dumped him and had pleaded with Sargent not to beat it.

Pat Volpondo, wherever he was now, would be laughing about the sorrel stallion — if that were the cause of his death. Sargent settled down in the chair, pushing for the morning to come sooner.

He was first consciously aware of the flame, but it was the sound that awakened him. Twice again, as he was diving toward a corner, he saw the flaming orange color and heard the shocking blast of gunpowder. A bedspring sang a weird complaint. Someone ran across the walk outside the window. Boots splashed in the sandy street. The footsteps receded rapidly.

Sargent was left crouched in a corner, his ears ringing, his nostrils full of powder stink. By the time he leaned from the window with his pistol in his hand, dogs were barking. There were no other sounds. He saw lamplight spring up in Tallman's office. Another light bloomed across the street in the Burent house.

All the dogs in town were baying now. Coyotes at the edge of town took it as a challenge and sent back their quavering calls.

Someone came thumping down the hall and began to beat on the door. "Sargent! You all right?"

It was Theobold. The man could get excited.

"I'm here. I shot at a coyote, yapping in the street."

There was a pause. Theobold tried the door. It was locked. "A coyote?"

"Three times. I missed. Go back to bed."

Theobold stopped rattling the door. "I wasn't in bed." He spoke like a rebuffed child. Presently he walked down the hall.

Someone leaned from an upstairs window. It sounded like Hitchcock's voice. "What the hell's going on down there?"

"Go to bed," Sargent said. He dragged the rocker into a corner and sat down again, with his gun lying on the floor beside him.

Voices began to churn in the lobby, coming indistinctly to Sargent. Sheriff Tallman asked a question. Theobold answered profanely, and Tallman laughed. Then, after several minutes, the lobby was still again. The mutter of voices at an upstairs window stopped. Weston was quiet except for one dog with a shrill yip. A few moments later the dog yelped, and everything was still.

Sargent stretched his feet out. It was not worth the struggle to pull his boots off over blistered skin. Some time later he slept. . . .

Chapter Five

No one had been in the scrub oak thicket under Antoro Pass since Sargent had left it the day before. The heat was there, the disturbed ant hill, and the broken branches.

Ulysses Morton swung down from a stocky gray, and stood a moment, watching Sargent. At breakfast the liveryman had asked to go along. There were three horses in the stable now since Sheriff Tallman had taken his at dawn to ride toward the lava.

Morton stuffed a rumpled gray shirt deeper under his belt, rubbing his lean stomach with his hand. He wore no pistol. "We're about a mile from Theobold's old place," he said.

"What does that mean?"

"Nothing. I always like to locate things."

Sargent went below the trail. No marks. The sorrel stallion must have lunged on down the trail after its dragging burden broke loose.

"I was over the back trail once to where it ran into the cattle tracks," Sargent said. "You want to bring the horses along slow on the trail while I walk that ground again?"

"All right."

Sargent found little that he had not seen the day before, a bit of fabric here and there, smeared against the rocks, dull stains where the ants were crawling thickly. The stallion had run like a crazy horse. Already the tracks looked old, heat-sloughed, growing dim. *They were old,* Sargent thought. Yesterday and the days before were gone forever.

He came out on the trail where he had quit the day before. Morton had left the horses. Now he was sitting on a rock, looking down to where the three main forks of the Sweetwater disappeared in a cañon.

"Nothing." Sargent took off his hat and wiped his forehead. The blisters on his feet were broken now. "Does it ever cool off here?"

"Not too much. Good climate for growing things." Morton kept looking down at the Sweetwater.

Growing things. Sargent looked at the blistered rocks and the scrubby aspens. There was grass, all right, wherever there was soil. "I want to watch both sides of the trail from here on," he said.

Morton held out Windy's reins. "I'll take

the upper side. All right?"

"Fine."

They walked slowly with Sargent in the lead. After a hundred yards Sargent shook his head at Morton. He raised one boot and wiggled it, and then he swung into the saddle.

"You should have soaked those feet," Morton said.

They rode slowly, leaning out with one hand on the horn. Several times they stopped and got down when the sign beside the trail was obscure, and every time it was the tracks of catch dogs that had flanked the herd. The trail itself was a winding, dusty puddle of hoof marks. The cattle that had chopped it were now rocking over iron in a slatted railroad car. Like the yesterdays, they were gone for good.

About a half mile from where they had started riding, Sargent held up his hand and stopped. Morton rode in beside him. Below them, where the rocks made a tiny basin clotted with bunch grass, were marks that had not come from catch dogs. They stayed on the rocks, circling the little depression, squatting to look down at the sign. A horse had spun and threshed in the little basin, struggling to break downhill. It had reared and scored the sides of rocks with steel, and then it had gone back to the trail.

"A rope on it . . . from the trail," Morton said.

Sargent nodded. He jumped down and moved carefully over the ground. So did Morton. Caught in the grainy roughness of a rock was a small bunch of sorrel hairs. On another rock he found a dull spot that might have been blood from a scraped leg. Sargent found nothing more.

"His pistol was gone," Morton said.

"Uhn-huh." That could have been taken on the trail, or it could have been knocked a long ways from the route the stallion had taken, after it left the trail.

They went back to the horses. Sargent got down on his hands and knees, but there was nothing left to read on the trail. For an hour he and Morton searched among the rocks on both sides of the cattle tracks. If a man had been waiting for Volpondo, he had gone and come by leaping from rock to rock — and they could find no evidence of that.

"Boots will knock a few white spots in this rotten granite," Morton said. "It ain't been done."

Once more they returned to the horses. Sargent watched the animals stamp, swing their necks, and whisk their tails at flies.

"Let's lead 'em up on the trail about ten feet."

Morton was puzzled. He said nothing. After the horses had been led away, they sat in the shade of the rocks and waited. Sargent filled his pipe and was starting to scratch a match when he rose and walked back slowly to where the animals had been. Morton followed.

Flies were scurrying across the ground. There was a little clot of them digging in the dust. Sargent raked his fingers through the dirt and came up with a piece that was caked together with brown. Flies settled on it as he held it in his hand. Morton also raked the trail with his fingers. Together, the two men found several bits of brown-caked dirt.

"The cattle were moving," Morton said. "One might have banged up a leg or had a torn nose from a catch dog." He shook his head. "No cow stopped long enough to lose more'n a few drops of blood."

Sargent brought Windy back to the place. He mounted and uncoiled his rope. "Walk down in the little hole, will you?"

He put his loop on Morton there, below the trail, in an easy throw. Startled, Windy braced for the unexpected tension, then looked around inquiringly when Morton

61

threw the loop off, and Sargent began to snake the rope back.

"Not so easy on a running horse," Sargent said. "But it could have been done."

Morton said: "From what I've seen of that stallion's tracks, it would take a powerful roping horse to hold him."

"It was done." Sargent was bleak with the knowledge of what he had hoped would not be so — someone had killed Pat Volpondo at this spot. The stallion had gone downhill in a great leap. The man had roped it, held it, finally forced it back to the trail.

"You saw a rope burn on his ankle, Morton?"

The liveryman came back to the trail. "No doubt. Manila fibers ground in."

Cold horror ran through Sargent. Pat might have been alive when someone tied his foot into the stirrup — first roped out of the saddle but still alive. He would not have asked for any favors. He would have lain there on the ground and. . . .

Sargent's hand was trying to crush the saddle horn. His flat-cheeked face had lost its habitual gravity.

Morton said quickly: "We'd best find out where the ambusher was hidden. It wasn't from the rocks or the man wouldn't have been here quick to rope as he passed."

Sargent stared at the gray man. "I don't remember ever mentioning to you that Pat rode a stallion."

Morton's eyes did not change. "Tallman mentioned it this morning when he got his horse. I ride the rocks a lot. He said to keep an eye out for a sorrel stallion, about twelve hundred, maybe with a rig still on it."

"I'm sorry."

"I know how you feel, Sargent. I knew when you led your horse down to the burying ground yesterday." Morton looked up the trail. "Would your friend have been hard to take by a man meeting him on the trail?"

"Damned hard. I'm wondering what he was doing on this trail."

"It goes on through to Turret," Morton said. "Few riders ever use Antoro to cross the Emigrants."

"Let's look ahead."

They found what they wanted to know not fifty yards ahead. Oak brush choked a narrow opening between two leaning rocks. Behind it a horse had waited. It had come through with a lunge, leaving strands of gray hair clinging to the brush.

Sargent faced Windy into the place, and then he had to go on through to turn. From the saddle, looking through the dust-pale leaves, he could see the spot where

Volpondo must have fallen.

"He came out with a rush as he passed," Morton said. "Maybe he figured on the stallion breaking straight ahead. At any rate he was able to get it back here."

No attempt had been made to cover sign. The tying to the stirrup had been either the act of a hellish mind or something done in vengeance. Sargent felt the cold twisting inside again, but this time he controlled it and harnessed it to his purpose.

Back on the trail he laid strands of horse hair against the shoulder of Morton's gray. After a time he decided the hairs did not match. Morton watched silently.

"You know the horses that are regularly around this country, don't you, Morton?"

The gray man stared toward the faraway Sodas, pale and ghostly beyond the shimmering lava plain. "I wouldn't guess about a thing like that. Sometimes the hair from one horse sticks to the sheepskin of the skirts and comes loose when the saddle is on another horse. You know that, Sargent."

"I know that this hair came off the shoulders or the rump of a gray horse that crashed out of the brush."

Morton nodded. "So it appears. Like I say, I wouldn't want to make any guesses."

Sargent gave him a long look. Morton

shook his head stubbornly. "I wouldn't make any loose guesses."

"Where's the Triangle Y and Anchor from here?"

"I'll show you."

Morton swung up. He was sure active for a middle-aged man. Sargent felt his grayness wasn't deep.

They went among tall aspen. Sargent heard the rushing of a creek ahead and soon they stopped in it.

"East Fork of the Sweetwater," Morton said. "Where Tallman said you figured on settling. Theobold's got it pretty well sewed up, but he'll never do anything with it."

"Whitey Fallon said this was Triangle range."

"They use it. Theobold don't give a hang. None of this is much good for cattle, Sargent."

It looked all right to Sargent, but now he did not care. He looked at the fine white scales at the base of the gelding's mane hairs, and then on down at the leaping water. He thought of all the times he and Pat Volpondo had stopped together to water their horses in streams just like this. Those memories would have to be pushed behind him now, for they would be knife-edged as long as the man who had killed Volpondo rode free. Alma Burent had called it vengeance. He did not like the word, and neither was it justice in his mind. It was simply a job that a man must do.

"You're not as old as you act sometimes, are you?" Morton asked.

"I'm twenty-eight."

Volpondo had been twenty-eight two weeks ago. They had been eighteen when Clay Sargent died, and they had discovered that the ranch was one mortgage on top of another. The day after Ben's funeral they had made their pact to own their own ranch in ten years. *I said I would not look back any more,* Sargent told himself.

Windy was faking now, nuzzling at the water, pretending to drink. "Get out of that," Sargent said. With his head still down, Windy splashed on across the stream.

A few rods farther on little aspens were closing in on two unfinished cabins. The larger cabin had been started with tremendous yellow pine logs, the ends projecting five feet from the corners. The large structure was set quartering west, commanding a view of the brown lava plain, the Soda Mountains, and the rugged Emigrant range.

"Theobold was going to ranch once," Morton said. "The boom in the Sodas collapsed, and so did Tracy." Morton's tone was touched with bitterness and contempt.

An hour more toward the west they came to a fork in the trail. Morton pointed ahead. "That way to Turret." He turned right, and presently Sargent heard the booming of another creek. "The Middle Fork," Morton said. "Between here and the West Fork . . . that comes from Turret . . . Cripple Creek is the only other stream of any size. Anchor's on it."

"Who owns Anchor?"

"Tug Marshall. Gin Carstairs runs it. Tug ain't been here for two years. He's over the hill, getting doctored." Morton spat. "This is Anchor's last roundup. Fletcher Hitchcock is taking the place over this winter."

From the top of a rocky crest Sargent caught a fleeting glimpse of stone buildings in a narrow green park to the west. They came to the Middle Fork and followed it. A trail forked to the west, about where Sargent estimated they should turn to go toward the buildings they had seen.

Morton went straight on down the stream. "I hear you sort of called Pete Weston last night," he said.

"He's touchy."

"You said it right. Pete don't forget."

"I guessed that."

"Remember it."

They had crossed the stream twice before Sargent asked: "What were the stone buildings to the west?"

"Triangle."

"And Anchor is west of there?"

"Uhn-huh."

"We're riding north," Sargent said.

"It ain't much out of the way to what I want you to see."

Not long afterward they stopped at the edge of a cañon. A cool wind was rising from where the river ran three hundred feet below. Windy sniffed and humped and backed away, rolling at the bit.

Morton was a different man. His eyes had brightened; his movements were brisk. He dismounted, stood on the edge of the wall, and motioned for Sargent to come over.

"See that shelf that runs along this wall, almost from the edge of the water?" Morton did not wait for an answer. "For nearly a mile that shelf is almost unbroken. You can ride a horse along it. It's just about water grade, Sargent. There is the Middle Fork and the East Fork. They don't flood much, like the West Fork. They're cutting all the timber near Turret now. Right down there is the place for the dam. You can take all the water along the ledge, and after that a California scraper will do the job, clear to the piñon mesas above Weston."

"I see," Sargent said without interest — or even feigned interest.

Morton went on rapidly. "Those piñon mesas will grow fruit like anything. I've had the soil tested. I got two wagon loads of it that I used to set a tree in my freight yard. That one tree produces peaches by the basket. You didn't see me water it this morning, did you?"

"No." *Morton was like a prospector,* Sargent thought, *only this was water and peaches.*

"There's room for twenty good orchards on those mesas. Think what that would do for Weston! Cattle, hell! Ranching is worn out here, Sargent. Tug Marshall knew it, or he would never have sold the Anchor. Sure, the Triangle can go on for quite a spell, using Theobold's graze and what they'll get from Anchor."

Morton was cutting the air with his hands, gesturing at the country. "Nine years ago the Sodas looked like they were loaded with gold. I started a freight business that would have made me rich . . . if things had lasted. Weston was booming. We started the new courthouse. We started the big reservoir you and I passed on the hill this morning. We did a lot of things, and then the strike blew sky high."

Morton shook his head violently. "Turret, sure. That's really a camp. It's only six years old. I didn't think it would last three months, or I might be a rich man today . . . me and Theobold, too. We got our bellies full on the Sodas deal. We had property out there, too damned much of it. There was a mining exchange in Weston, fourteen saloons. You couldn't fight your way into the Lava House at night."

Morton stabbed his finger toward the cañon. "That stuff down there will last forever, Sargent. Put it on those mesas and you've done something. Trees keep growing. They get old, you plant a new one. Take gold out of the ground, and it's gone. It don't grow back. I got interested right after the blow-up in the Sodas. I got Theobold interested, too. We started a dam, but we started too late in the winter and below the junction of all three rivers. We put every cent we had left into it."

Morton shook his head. "High water, mostly from the West Fork, took everything out in the spring. Theobold quit cold. He runs by fits and starts anyway. Three years ago he thought he was going to raise some money from friends back East, but it went foul some way . . . and after that he lost all interest."

Three years before, a gang had dynamited an express car at Costilla Pass, and that deal had turned foul on the robbers, too. Sargent stared down into the cañon, not seeing anything at all.

"I. . . ." Morton noticed Sargent's abstraction. "Well, I'll ride back toward the Triangle with you."

The life had gone from his voice. Morton mounted his gray. Once more he was a lean, middle-aged man without any apparent interest in anything but the moment.

"Your idea sounds all right to me," Sargent said.

"Does it?" Morton's eyes brightened, and then he saw that Sargent had been speaking honestly, no more than that. "Yeah. Good idea. I've bothered people with it before, Sargent."

Where the trail forked toward Triangle, Sargent paused once he saw Morton was not turning.

"I'm not welcome over there," Morton said. "Old Hitchcock thinks I want to flood the country with farmers."

Morton most likely had given the Triangle owner a fit over putting up money for the peach project. A dream was all right. Sargent had nursed one along — until yesterday. He could understand Morton's feelings, and for a moment Sargent wished he were a man who could smooth things over with words.

He said: "Thanks, Morton," and watched the gray man ride toward the Emigrants again. Morton had not asked a question about the excitement last night. Neither had Tallman. The coyote story had not fooled anyone.

Morton's gray disappeared among the aspens along the noisy creek. He was going straight toward where he and Sargent had been that morning. *I wonder why?* Sargent asked himself.

Chapter Six

Triangle was set in a narrow park, hemmed by rocky crests on all sides. The buildings had been put there to stay. The corrals were solid, their corners bastions of rock and mortar. There were a dozen horses in one corral, more grazing in a meadow above the ranch buildings. *A relatively small range,* Sargent thought. *They could handle everything on roundup right from here.*

He stopped before the cook shack. A moon-faced man with droopy eyes stuck his head out. "Light down and have a bite, mister."

The cook shack was cleaner than many Sargent had seen and the cook more reticent. The two men said nothing while Sargent ate. One glance at the stove showed that some of the crew, at least, were expected back for dinner. Long habit forced Sargent away from the table quickly once he had eaten. He stood in the doorway, filling his pipe.

Across the yard, in the deep shade of a low-roofed porch around the main house, he saw a woman come to the door and look at his horse, and then she turned back into the house.

"Rustling for a job?" the cook asked.

"Not exactly."

The cook let it go at that. "The boss will be back about dinner time, I reckon."

"Thanks for the grub."

Sargent walked across the yard. He stood by the horse corral. Most of the horses would go around nine hundred, wiry animals suited for quick work among the rocks. There were two grays, one a short-packed powerhouse. The little wisps of hair in Sargent's pocket just might match that one.

He walked to the opposite corner of the corral and looked into the meadow. There was nothing there of the color he wanted. It occurred to him that bad manners and possible trouble were involved in fooling with another man's horse, but he ducked between the corral logs and moved slowly among the horses. The smaller gray was too light of color. He laid his strands of hair against the big brute's shoulder. It was pretty close, mighty close, but, as Morton had said, a man would want to be sure about a thing like that.

"Are you figuring on buying the bunch?"

Sargent jerked his head up, looking across

the back of the horse at a girl who had come to the corral bars. *Golden,* he thought. Golden hair with sun-lightened streaks and a light tan with freckles in it. He slipped the loose hairs into his pocket. "I fancy this one."

"So does Pete Weston. You'd better get out of there, mister. . . . Not that I care a bit, but Pete once half killed a man for slapping his horse over to make room at a hitch rack."

Sargent squeezed between the logs again. The girl was tall. Her eyes were a deep shade of green. Her appraisal carried a man's directness, but it left no doubt that the tally was figured in a woman's terms.

"You must be the man who came over Antoro yesterday."

Sargent nodded.

"Oh, yes. Whitey Fallon said you mentioned taking over some of Theobold's rock and timber claims."

"I guess I did."

She took his arm. It startled him a little, and the muscles above his elbow jerked. "Then you're Sargent, the man who shoots at coyotes under his window." She laughed.

"You get the news, I see."

"Clum Brand rode by early this morning. He was in Weston last night."

They walked to the house. The cook

75

peered from his shack, his round face expressionless. He spat and went inside again.

"I'm Monica Hardin," the girl said. "Hitchcock's niece by marriage. Poor relation. I cause Uncle Fletcher trouble all the time." She was walking close to Sargent, with the lithe stride of a young goat. "What else do they say about me in town?"

She was not talking fliply. She was making statements. Sargent looked at her sidewise. "I heard you caused Hitchcock to run his son off the place."

"That was Wayne's decision. He wanted to marry me. Uncle Fletcher said we were too young. They quarreled, and Wayne left." She held onto his arm until they were on the porch. "We were too young, I suppose." It was plain that the quarrel had not mattered much to her.

Sargent would have taken a chair near the stone coping of the porch. She guided him instead to a long, hide-covered seat suspended on chains. *A good cutting horse could not have done a better job on a clumsy steer,* he thought as he sat down beside her.

"So we're going to have another ranch here, Mister . . . what's your first name?" She smoothed her gingham dress over the contours of long legs. She punched the porch with the tips of her toes, and the seat began to swing a little.

"Brock. I've changed my mind about ranching."

"You could still go to work for Triangle. You'd like it here, Brock."

He had seen flirts. They had bothered him because he was a self-contained man, naturally reserved — a Gloomy Gus, Pat Volpondo used to say. Little, laughing Pat, when the two of them had been together. . . .

"I didn't scare you, did I?" Monica was watching his face. "I only said you'd like it here."

Sargent went back to his first thought. *No, she did not annoy him. She was forthright in her flirting, if that's what it was. There was no guile in her eyes, but yet a man could not look at her and forget she was a woman.* He said: "I've thought some of rustling a job here even after I told Fallon no yesterday." He had changed his mind down there at the corral when he matched color on a gray horse.

A middle-aged woman came to the door with a dish towel in her hands. She was heavy set with graying hair pulled into a knot at the back of her neck. She merely glanced at Sargent and then looked steadily at Monica.

"A new rider, Missus Sommers," Monica said. It was explanation and dismissal.

"Uhn-huh," the woman said, and walked away.

"Do you get many new riders here?" Sargent asked.

"Too few." Monica pushed the seat again. "They don't get along well with Chuck and Pete."

"I thought Fallon was the foreman."

"He is."

Sargent filled in the rest easily enough. "Whitey is pretty handy with that pistol he carries in his chaps. He put it on me yesterday when I surprised him in the rocks."

"You're lucky he didn't shoot. It's been only in the last year that Triangle and Anchor cattle stopped wandering into Turret butcher shops by the dozens. Whitey Fallon still carries a little lead he earned stopping that. Anytime you meet him in the rocks, he'll look you over from behind a piece of steel."

"Speak of the devil," Sargent murmured.

Fallon, Chuck Ozanne, Weston, and a tall, lean man with a white mustache were riding up the creek. Three huge, shaggy catch dogs were pacing the horses. Sargent went over to the porch coping and sat down.

Weston's blocky face was turned toward

the porch all the time he was riding past on his way to the corrals. Fallon nodded. Ozanne and the tall oldster came over to the porch. The lean man would have to be Hitchcock. His features were the same as the express messenger's, the bold jutting nose, the blue eyes, the lines at the corners of the nose.

Hitchcock swung down. Monica introduced Sargent. The old man looked from the girl to Sargent and then to Ozanne. He shook hands without enthusiasm.

Ozanne had not dismounted. With a half smile on his dark face he said: "Why'd you shift from the swing, Sargent?"

"Shut up, Chuck," Hitchcock said.

"I'm looking for a job," Sargent said.

Hitchcock nodded. He studied the younger man, and it seemed to Sargent that the old boy liked his looks. "You turned Whitey down yesterday, Sargent."

"I changed my mind."

Hitchcock glanced at Monica. "I don't need a man right now."

"You said this morning you needed two more men, Uncle Fletch."

"Changed my mind," Hitchcock said.

Ozanne looked down at the neck of his pinto, one side of his mouth twisted in a smile. He swung his right foot free of the

79

stirrup and rested it on the porch corner coping. Sargent gave quick, hard attention to the light patches on the shoulders of the horse.

"Why did you change your mind, Uncle Fletch?"

The weariness on Hitchcock's face seemed to come from an old pattern. "You know damned well why, girl. He's not old enough or near ugly enough." He started toward the door. With a hand on the latch he paused, hesitating over something. Whatever the warring matter was, he took the short end of it, and his face was lined with resignation. "Eat with us, son," he said to Sargent. "Then try Anchor."

Hitchcock stamped caked mud from his boots and went inside. "Missus Sommers," he called. "Missus Sommers."

Ozanne looked at Sargent with amused insolence. "Sit down in the swing again, Sargent. You won't hurt anything." He smiled at Monica, and then he put his foot in the stirrup and spurred toward the corrals.

Pete Weston was stamping toward the porch, his rolling gait sending little jets of dust from his bootheels. Ozanne asked a question. Weston paid no attention. Ozanne leaped down, slapped the pinto toward the corrals, and came walking back toward the house.

Weston's mouth hung open as he stared at Sargent. "Are you the one that went in and out of the horse corral?"

Monica said: "No, Pete!" and at the same time Sargent nodded.

"You had your guts, didn't you?" Weston moved over to the steps. "Come off there, Sargent, or. . . ."

"It's my business, Pete," Fallon came up with Ozanne. The foreman's eyes were cold. "I sized you up as a man who's been around, Sargent. I thought you had better sense than to fool around horses that didn't belong to you."

"I had a reason."

"That's why I'm here," Fallon said. "Give it."

Sargent took the hairs from his shirt pocket. "These came off the horse of a rider who killed a man below Antoro Pass two days ago. They match that big gelding in. . . ."

"By God!" Weston roared. He started up the steps, and Whitey's sharp order did not check him.

"Pete!" Hitchcock was standing in the doorway. Weston took two more steps before he stopped, with anger and obedience

81

making an ugly struggle on his face.

"He accused me of killing a man!" Weston appealed to Hitchcock, and pointed at Sargent. "Last night he said. . . ."

"Be quiet, Pete." Hitchcock looked at Sargent. "I see now. You're another of the bunch that's bothered us to death since the robbery in Weston. You intended to plant yourself at Triangle as a spy."

"No, he didn't," Monica said.

"Be quiet!" With Weston, Hitchcock had been strong, without anger, but his voice directed at the woman rose and nearly cracked with rage.

"Whatever I had in mind," Sargent said, "I would like to know who rode that big gray day before yesterday . . . and where."

Weston's chest was heaving under his sweat-soaked blue shirt. The whole big animal smell and the anger of him were strong on the shaded porch. "Last night he said Clum and me was blind. Today he says. . . ."

"Well?" Hitchcock was looking at Fallon.

"I sent Pete up the Middle Fork to the Horseshoe Rocks." Fallon's blistered face was expressionless. "That's where I sent him two days ago."

"And that's where you rode, Pete?" Hitchcock asked.

Weston started to shout, and then he nodded.

"From what I've heard, that's a long way
from where you found this dead man, Sargent." Hitchcock's eyes were level, no
longer friendly. "Pete's answer is good
enough for me. I think you'd better accept
it, too."

Weston started to unbuckle his gun belt.

Hitchcock shook his head.

"He called me a liar, Fletch. I got a right
to. . . ."

"Triangle is unhappy enough without a
fist fight in the yard," Hitchcock said. His
glance brushed the woman standing behind
Sargent, and then he said to Sargent: "You
fellows that work for the express company
have a job to do, I've no doubt. To me, it's
dirty undercover sort of work, and I think
a man like you could find a better job.
That's your business, Sargent. I withdraw
the invitation to eat."

"I never said the dead man I found had
anything to do with the express company
robbery, Hitchcock."

"It is reasonable for me to assume as
much." Hitchcock looked at Sargent's horse
near the cook shack.

Sargent put the horse hairs into his
pocket. He buttoned the flap, staring gravely

at the Triangle owner. "I may have to come back."

"I can't refuse you that," Hitchcock said. "Though you won't be welcome." He looked once more at Weston, and then he went into the house.

Monica walked across the yard with Sargent. Ozanne followed. He began to wash at a bench outside the door of the cook shack.

"Come back anytime," Monica said.

"You heard what your uncle said, Monica." Ozanne was soaping his hands.

"*That's* what he said, Brock." She smiled. "Ride in anytime you like."

"Thanks." Sargent smiled down at the girl with one eye on Ozanne. The slender, handsome man was trying to smile, but Sargent read on his face all the uncertainty and hell that a jealous man in love can suffer.

"Do you always wash before you put your horse away, Ozanne?" Sargent asked. "But since you've started, let me put the pinto in for you. I'd like to check those light gray patches on his shoulders."

"Don't try it!"

"I thought you might say that." Sargent touched his hat to Monica, got on his horse, and rode across the yard without haste. Ozanne watched him all the way. The girl went back toward the porch with a lithe stride. Old Hitchcock had come out again and was standing with one hand on a post. He did not appear as ramrod straight as he had been before.

Hitchcock could handle men, all right, but he had another problem that was biting his insides. Monica went up the steps and into the house. Hitchcock did not glance at her.

When Sargent turned the corner of the horse corral, Fallon spoke carefully. "You got too many guts for your own good, mister. Know what I mean?"

"Be sure that big gray was where you thought it was two days ago, Whitey."

Sargent left the Triangle foreman as he had left him two days before, standing with his head lowered into his shoulders like a contemplative lobo.

Chapter Seven

Turret was hell's broth with the boiling sounds intact. Tunnel dumps crowded the town, and the town crowded the gulch, and the voices of the inhabitants battered at the Emigrants. Men walked where there was room. There was more room in the streets than on the walks, so teamsters and other drivers did the best they could.

Sargent let Windy pick the way up the long main street. Men banged against the stirrups, cursing or grinning at Sargent as the blue roan cleaved steady passage. Traffic in and out of nine or ten saloons that Sargent passed made cross currents in the general flow. Sargent ducked tatters from a bullet-ripped canvas sign that spanned the street, proclaiming **The Finest Gents Clothing In The West**. He glanced toward the galloping white horse sign of Western Express in the window of a narrow office. Fresh brown paint gleamed on the facings of false pillars before the marshal's office. Bold lettering on the window said **Marty Packard**, and beneath it in six-inch letters was **City Marshal**.

Sargent broke clear of the seething core of the town at last, coming to a section dominated by liveries and freight yards. He rode on past, sizing up the stacks of baled hay, eyeing the conditions of the livery stables; and then he stopped a six-horse teamster coming into town.

"Which is the best place for a good horse?"

The teamster spat. He looked at Windy, and then looked at Sargent. His own horses were sleek and gleaming, with rosettes on the headstalls and scarlet pompons bobbing between their ears. "Bayhead's," he said, and looked Windy over again.

Sargent had picked the place himself. He was pleased to find his judgment confirmed. The warm and not unpleasant smells of a stable interior came with the squat man who reached out to take Windy's reins at the doors. The man grinned hugely.

"Brock-ee!" His handclasp was as solid as the shoulder of a horse.

"Three years, Benny. A long time to go without that wine of yours." The grave lines of Sargent's face broke.

Benny Paez looked into the street. "And thee Patrick with thee devil's grin . . . ? You are not here without heem?"

Paez was part of the past. He had raised kids and vegetables on the Alder Creek bottom when Sargent was a boy. His guitar and songs and wine, his pungent tales of revolutions below the border — all these had held Sargent and Volpondo many an evening under the locust trees at Paez's farm. It was said in the Alder country that Paez was a *good* Mexican. He minded his business. He paid his bills.

What Paez saw on Sargent's features put Indian flatness into the hosteler's own face. He led the blue roan to a stall. Together they took care of the horse, and then they walked again.

"Pat is dead," Sargent said.

Paez's word was a long breath. *"¡Ai!"*

"His horse dragged him."

Paez's eyes glittered. He made a small motion of disagreement, a bare shake of his head. "I would like to see such a horse, Brock-ee, but there ees none."

"After he was roped from his horse and tied to the stirrup."

The hosteler's face was ugly and still. "We weel keel somebody now?" It was instant, elemental. All those stories about his part in revolutions had not been entertaining tales, Sargent knew.

"You didn't happen to see Pat come through here two days ago?"

Paez shook his head. "He would have

come to see me. He knew I am here."

"Did you know he worked for Western Express?"

"That could not be. He was always at Trinchera."

"He did. That's what got him killed."

"We weel start weeth what you have found out, and we weel keel someone," Paez said. "You know sometheeng?"

"Nothing . . . except that he was killed. Someone thought he was still working for the express company."

"*¡Ai!* The beeg safe stealing!"

Sargent nodded. "When the express agent here was shot, there were two men involved. One was killed. I'm wondering about the other one. You have friends here?"

"I have frens. Come for planning to my house tonight." He told Sargent where it was. "We weel talk about thees theeng. We weel sharpen knives."

"You have children, Benny?"

"They are grown."

"There is your wife."

"She sometimes quarrels weeth me because I did not mak a fortune in thee mines." Paez shrugged. "Where Mexicans cannot work, Brock-ee."

"Tonight we will talk about it."

Sargent liked Benny Paez, trusted him,

but it would not be fair to get him involved deeply into what now appeared to be the toughest job Sargent had ever tackled.

Marty Packard was giving orders to two deputies when Sargent entered the office of the city marshal.

"Tear it down," Packard said. "Every would-be tough in town takes shots at it."

"But the man says he paid. . . ."

"Tear the sign down!"

The deputies hurried out. Packard was young, rangy. His features were mainly a long, thin nose and hard green eyes. Even with his chair tipped back and his feet on the desk he carried an explosive look. His voice was harsh.

"What's your story, cowboy? Somebody steal your bridle?"

"A little worse than that. Last Monday night when someone shot the express agent. . . ."

"You want to know where Monte Bledsoe is . . . ? Why did I chase him out of town, huh? Didn't I realize the shooting was a fake?" Packard jerked his head impatiently. "Why don't you guys go down on the desert and dig up that safe? There never was anything here to help, or I would have smelled it out a long time ago."

Packard undoubtedly was tough. He

might even be as smart as the next man, but most likely he had too much of the first and too little of the second and one day would get himself prime for carrying on a door in Turret.

"Why did you chase Bledsoe, Marshal?"

Packard gave a great sigh of false patience. "Him and Drew Weaver had trouble before. They got to blasting last Monday evening. Weaver shot a horse dead, and then he nicked the express agent. Bledsoe just shot Weaver. I don't like trouble in my town . . . what's the name?"

"Sargent."

"Where from?"

"Weston."

Packard laughed. "I don't like trouble in my town, Sargent. I gave Bledsoe five minutes to slope. He took two."

"By then you knew about the robbery in Weston?"

"No, I didn't know! And it wouldn't have made any difference to me. Your boss wired me to hold the men involved in the shooting. I'd already run Bledsoe out of town. If I'd had Mike Hanawalt's wire to hold him, I still would have chased Bledsoe. I'm the marshal here, Sargent."

"Then you think the agent was shot accidentally?"

"I know it! Weaver got a horse, a window, and the express agent with about four shots." Packard took an expensive-looking cigar from his desk. "Wrong tree, Sargent. I wish you guys would go find the safe and leave me alone." Packard left the band on the cigar. He lit it, throwing the match over his shoulder. "That sheriff you got down there handled things like a Chinese fire drill. He went in every direction but the right one before he even knew what happened." Packard blew smoke. "How long do you Weston people think you're going to hog the courthouse, Sargent? We pay all the county taxes up here, you know."

Packard fancied himself already as sheriff of Weston County, Sargent thought. Any problem, viewed from the marshal's standpoint, must appear quite simple.

"You're from Weston?" Packard frowned. "The company wouldn't have any special agents there. Oh, I see . . . old Tallman's deputy, eh?"

"No," Sargent said. "Not an express company agent or a deputy sheriff." He started out.

Packard took his feet off the desk. "Hey! Who do you work for?"

"Brock Sargent, Marshal."

Chapter Eight

The desk clerk at the Swampscott House was a thin man behind a blue ascot tie. He might have had his opinion concerning Sargent's clothes, but he had been in the town long enough to know that any pocket could be full of gold.

"We have only a suite left . . . sir."

"All right."

"Twenty-five dollars."

"I didn't ask."

"No, sir," the clerk said quickly. His values were in order again. He pushed the register around.

Seafood, birds — any meat a man could ask for — was on the Swampscott menu. Sargent took a steak. It came under a silver dome, piping hot. Sargent looked gravely at the waiter. "Is this stolen beef from the Weston country?"

"No, sir! I'm sure it is not, sir. Our beef is all shipped in from Alder. That is, I'm sure it is."

Marty Packard came through the wide doors. He had changed his clothes. Polished boots, gray trousers, a red sash around his middle. His pistol was under a long black coat. *A gentleman marshal,* Sargent thought.

Packard's eyes narrowed when he saw Sargent. He came over to the table. "You think you pulled something, don't you, cowboy, asking questions without any authority. Don't try anything in my town, Sargent."

Packard walked away, smiling when a well-dressed man at a distant table waved his hand. Sargent saw him bow and join a group that appeared to be composed of mine owners and their wives. Sargent chewed his food slowly and watched the marshal.

A tough boy, trying to ride high, Packard was a man with whom you could get along fine in a cow camp, probably; but now he was out of his class. They weren't fawning on him over there; they were being patronizing, showing him off. Money made the difference. Packard was smart enough to realize that much, and now and then it seemed to Sargent that the marshal's face did show that he knew he was sitting temporarily where he could not live.

Sargent thought of gaunt Morse Tallman down in Weston. Tallman would never cater to anyone. The cheerful clatter of the big dining room, the noisy pushing of vitality on the street outside annoyed Sargent for a moment. Perhaps there was more honesty in dying Weston and lost dreams such as Ulysses Morton held than there was in all this gouging frenzy in Turret town.

The marshal's voice was loud at times. His companions now and then looked sidewise at each other, and smiled. There was one sharp-featured, heavy-set man at the table who never seemed to smile. It occurred to Sargent that a large slice of one hundred thousand dollars would make a man like Packard feel that his social status was assured. It was not a hunch but a strong idea with roots in a dozen lesser ideas.

Sargent gave the waiter a two-dollar tip. For the first time in ten years he could throw money away, if he wanted to.

"I asked the chef, sir. All our beef comes from Alder, the Trinchera Ranch. The very best, sir."

"Thank you. I am relieved." The Trinchera — Pat Volpondo's memory sprang up everywhere, and it pushed at Sargent to sit no longer when a job was undone.

The Paez cabin was at the toe of a fast-growing tunnel dump. Sargent squinted up as a trammer eased his car against the end chock and sent muck rattling down. One day, when they moved track up there, the cabin would be doomed.

Bernice Paez enveloped Sargent with heavy arms and a peppery breath. "So long ago, Brock-ee, on thee good farm at Alder." She smiled and kissed his cheek. There had been eight little Paezes, all boys, and sometimes in those years long gone *Señora* Paez had said that Pat and Brock were also sons. She cried a little now. "Thee smiling one, thee little Patrick. . . ." She sat down and began to cry in earnest.

"*Basta,* fat one!" Benny was sitting at a table. There was a lamp before him, a bottle of red wine, and in the midst of the white oilcloth — two knives.

"That one!" *Señora* Paez pointed at her husband. "First, thee farm ees sold to buy paper een mines which are no good. And now he has thrown away hees job!"

"Next week thee cabin weel be covered," Benny said. "There weel be no place to live except behind thee stable. And now, woman, peace."

Paez was in for it. His wife looked at the knives on the table, and then she appealed to Sargent. He nodded.

"I have asked certain ones," Paez said. "Bledsoe and Weaver came here together, from where no one knows. They quarreled about a woman een thee Golden Bear. They fought, not dangerously, and thee marshal put them een jail. And then last Monday night they fought weeth guns. Weaver died. One horse was killed. Saddler, thee express agent, was shot een thee. . . ." Paez tapped his chest with powerful fingers.

Sargent put in: "Nicked, Packard said."

"Bledsoe was tol' to go away by Packard, but not unteel after Bledsoe had run away . . . and then returned late thee same night. Thees telling I heard myself een thee Teamsters' Bar." Paez stared at the knives. "Why did thees Bledsoe go away and then return?"

"I wonder. What did Packard say to Bledsoe?"

"To go away een" — Paez held up his hand — "five minutes or he would be dead. Bledsoe went queeckly. I got thee horse from thee stall for heem."

"What kind of horse?"

"A poor one. Red roan. A beaten animal that had back sores from a wrinkled blanket. It was een need of shoes." Paez passed the wine bottle. He drank after Sargent had drunk. "Thees Bledsoe has been back. One of my frens saw heem two nights ago."

"Does Packard know that?"

Paez shook his head. "Thee marshal knows what happens among those who own thee mines. That ees mostly what thee marshal knows."

"What kind of man is Packard?"

Paez smiled grimly. "He ees thee peon who would walk with thee *gachupines*."

Gachupines — wearers of shoes. In Paez's day in Mexico only the wealthy owned shoes.

"To steal thee gold in Weston eet was necessary that there be no agent here," Paez said. "Many know that. No one knows where thee gold ees. All Benny Paez knows ees that Pat Volpondo, our fren, ees now dead because of thee gold." He put wide fingers on a knife handle and stared at Sargent, then took a flat stone from his pocket and began to whet the steel. "Now, you weel tell me thee first one we weel keel."

Sargent glanced at *Señora* Paez, sitting by the stove, her back against the white-washed logs.

"First, we must know several things," Sargent said. "We must be sure that the agent, Saddler, was shot on purpose."

"There were two," Paez said. "They made to quarrel over a woman. They fought a leetle. Later, they were seen as frens. Still later, they quarrel again and thee agent ees shot. Eet was meant to shoot heem, and Weaver did not die by accident, either."

Paez shrugged. "There ees more to divide when there are fewer robbers. Thees Bledsoe had the look about heem, Brock-ee. He ees first?"

Paez tested steel with his thumb, then he spat on the stone, and went to work again.

"There are several involved."

"No matter. They all caused thee death of Patrick. All I ask ees who ees thee first?"

"If Bledsoe is what we think," Sargent said, "his trail will lead me to the others."

"Eet ees so . . . if thee others do not decide that Bledsoe ees another robber too many."

There were no kinks in Benny's thinking.

"Someone planned everything," Sargent said. "Before we chop limbs, we should find the trunk."

Paez stopped whetting his knife. His face was flat and dangerous. "Packard . . . ," he began.

Señora Paez struck her head with both hands. "He says that, Brock-ee, because *Señor* Packard threw heem een jail for fighting een a saloon!"

"His deputies beat me." Paez nodded. "I beat them a leetle also. Perhaps I am wrong about Packard, but yet. . . ."

"I think you are, Benny. The man who planned the robbery was a smart man." Sargent was turning ideas about Marty Packard and had been doing so all evening, but he did not want Benny's direct mind in the same channel. He wanted his friend to live a long life. "Shooting at a mud hen will scare away the mallards."

"Ah, *sí*," Paez said, "thee large canal where we hunted. Do you remember when Patrick pulled my little Juan and Diego from there, and Juan was dead . . . ?"

"No! No!" *Señora* Paez cried. "Eet ees not good to say that!"

"And Patrick spread hees knees beside thee legs of Juan, who was dead, and pushed thee life back eento heem after long working, while my wife cried, and I was helpless?"

"I remember," Sargent said.

"That ees only one theeng." Paez was whetting the second knife. "We have much to remember of Patrick. So perhaps I am too eager to slice thee large ducks. I will do then as you say, Brock-ee. What ees eet that you say?"

"Someone must watch here for Bledsoe. Who is this woman he will return to see?"

"Ginger at thee Golden Bear. She could scare a horse from a narrow trail. She ees thee one."

"You must find out also, if you can, how

it was known to Bledsoe that the safe was on the train. Tonight I will talk to this Ginger myself."

"You would keep me from being useful." Paez tested the knife. "But I said that I would do as you commanded, and so I weel."

"Good." Sargent rose. Paez put one of the knives in a goatskin sheath. Sargent took it, saying: "With the job gone, you will need money."

Benny shook his head.

Sargent gave banknotes to *Señora* Paez. She returned half of them. *"Basta,"* she said. "Enough to feed even a great plotter like Benny Paez."

"Where will you be after you see thees Ginger?" Paez asked.

"Tomorrow I ride back to Weston. The sheriff there will know where I am . . . most of the time. If there is big news, do not trust the telegraph. You can find a man to send?"

"Sí," Paez said. "Myself. . . ."

The herder at the Golden Bear leaned on the rail before the orchestra, a bored and listless man, but his voice was large. "The next dance will begin soon. We have beautiful ladies, gentlemen, and they are beautiful dancers! Pick out one of these bright-eyed fairies. . . ."

A face that would scare a horse on a narrow trail. Many of the "bright-eyed fairies" qualified. Sargent chose one at random. Her name was Lily. She began to take interest when she bumped against Sargent's money belt on the way to the bar. They had beer at fifty cents a bottle. Lily's beer was colored water, but it cost the same. The bartender gave her two tickets.

Sargent and Lily danced, and the woman made sure about the money belt. "I took you for a cowboy at first, handsome." The floor was packed, strong with human smells and other odors brought with celebrating teamsters. "I ain't seen you around, have I?"

"I generally dance at the Mountain Palace."

"Grace's place, huh? You don't mind getting robbed, do you?"

They danced twice more before Sargent said: "I don't see Ginger around. Isn't she working tonight?"

"You just bumped into her, handsome. The peroxide one, there, with the little whiskery geezer." Lily's eyes narrowed. After a few more bumps and shuffles she murmured, "Looking for Monte?"

Sargent changed his plans. He did not need Ginger. It had not been a good idea to talk to her in the first place. "Yes, I'd like to talk to Bledsoe. Seen him around lately?"

"I can't remember, offhand." Lily rubbed against the money belt. "Several men have asked about Monte."

"Twenty dollars?"

"Fifty," Lily said.

The fiddle player went off on a musical spree. The drummer got mad and tried to drown him out. "Remember," Sargent said.

They took their beer to a table this time. Sargent lifted a sleeping drunk, chair and all, and set him against the wall. The man fell on the floor, and the herder dragged him toward a back door. Sargent held Lily's hand, smiling at her. Then she fumbled with the V of her low gown and was fifty dollars richer.

"He came back two nights ago. Ginger thought she was sneaking out unseen when she talked to him on the back stairs. That Ginger. . . ." Lily forgot and sipped her colored water. "Gawd!" she said, and dropped the bottle on the floor. She took Sargent's beer and drank. "That Ginger, she's been putting on airs, talking mysteriously about getting out of this business."

"What does she say?"

"Just hints, la-de-dah stuff, and getting uppity with the rest of us."

"Who has talked to her lately?"

"Some good-looking strangers have weaseled around like you did and then danced with her." Lily stared at the crowded floor. "That didn't used to happen." Craft came down on Lily's face. "What do you want with Monte Bledsoe? Do you think he killed the express agent here to get him out of the way so them others could take the safe at Weston?"

Sargent shook his head. "Bledsoe killed Weaver, didn't he? Weaver is the one who put a wild slug into Saddler. I used to ride with Monte down in New Mexico and. . . ."

"There's a reward, ain't there . . . for the man and for the safe?"

"Forget the safe, Lily. I have other business with Bledsoe."

"I imagine. Let me tell you something, cowboy. Bledsoe hated Weaver's guts, after Weaver made a play for Ginger. Maybe Weaver didn't know he was going to get his in that frame-up that hurt the express agent . . . but Bledsoe knew it." Lily stared hard. "I oughta have more money."

"You might get it, depending on how

much news you can pick up from Ginger in the next few days. I'll be back then."

Lily looked Sargent over again. She was not thinking of his money belt. "Come anytime, handsome. Anytime."

"Has Packard ever come in to dance with Ginger?" Sargent asked.

"Him?" Lily snorted. "He's too good to dance here any more. He come in and talked to her a few days ago."

Ginger was running up the stairway when Sargent went out. He went up the street and around the corner. There was darkness then and no sidewalk. He felt, rather than saw, an alley that ran behind the Golden Bear. It would not hurt to get acquainted with that narrow passage.

He stumbled over cans and trash before he moved in against a wall, and then he smelled the feathery odor of ash piles disturbed by his boots. The Golden Bear was three stories high, the largest building in the block. He could see the bulk of it with lights from other buildings on the street trying to bend around the corners. A lamp went on in a corner room on the third floor of the Golden Bear, and then it was off again. Sargent thought his luck might be riding high, after all.

There was no warning. The blow came

from the darkness around the L of the next building, the smell of which advertised its status. One moment Sargent was feeling his way along. The next split second he was sitting in the alley, dazed. A man was running hard, kicking tin cans, splintering packing cases in his flight toward the end of the alley which Sargent had entered.

Then the man was gone. It was dead quiet in the alley, and the racket of the street came over the walls and through the walls. Sargent rose, almost falling a second time as a tin can rolled under his foot. He saw the light in the third-story room of the Golden Bear flare up again. This time it stayed on. He kept moving up the alley until he was almost under the light. He saw the dim outline of a stairway against the rear of the building, high up. Pawing at the blackness, he found a splintery rail. He stiffened when a door opened up there at the back of the dance hall. He heard the rustle of a woman's dress. A board creaked.

It was then that someone rammed a gun in his back. "Don't move."

Sargent's pistol was lifted expertly from its holster almost at the same instant. He heard it strike boards across the alley.

"Don't move at all," the man behind him said.

Upstairs, the dress rustled again. The door opened and shut quickly.

The man behind Sargent shifted his left hand to the pistol, and then the barrel was slanting into Sargent's back. A hand came up and felt his right ear. "Yeah," the man said under his breath. "I was afraid of that."

Sargent drove backward then, jamming his back against the slanting pistol barrel. At the same time he grabbed the hand at his ear. The pistol ripped the silence of the alley. With his legs spread Sargent bent his back, hurling the man behind him over his shoulder. The body crashed into the stair rail and broke it. The man rolled into a pile of cans.

The alley was quiet again. Upstairs, the bait was gone. Down here, Sargent had something to examine. At least, he had made contact. He kicked out gently with his feet until he felt the man's legs, and then he knelt beside him and lit a match.

It did not live long enough to burn back to the stick. All the lights in the world went out for Sargent, and this time he did not know anything at all.

Chapter Nine

The bunk was too narrow, and it had great lumps in the mattress. Sargent thought the fearful heat of the room must be adding to his feeling of nausea. Although the room was small and shadowy, there was light on Sargent's face. He saw it came from a small lamp with a shield. He could not fit the room to anything he knew. A great chimney ran up through it, and a fire was leaking a little rim of light from around an iron door in the bricks. He started to put his leg over the edge of the bunk.

"Just lie there, Sargent." The voice came from beside the chimney, from a narrow opening between the bricks and shelving that ran to the ceiling. It was not the voice Sargent had heard in the alley.

In another room, reached by a door at Sargent's left, he heard a man walk across the floor. Metal rang on metal. A grinding sound started.

"Your head clear now?" the voice asked.

Neither his head nor his future was as clear as Sargent would have liked. He tried to peer into the space between the chimney and the shelves. He could not see a thing except a pistol resting on a brace between the bricks and wood.

"I'll have to know what you're up to, Sargent."

"That makes a pair of us."

"You talked to Packard about Monte Bledsoe. You asked a girl in the Golden Bear about him. What do you want with Bledsoe?"

"Personal business," Sargent said. He felt for his money belt. It was gone.

"Yes, that's another strike on you, Sargent. You were carrying too much money for a drifting cowboy. Where did it come from?"

From ten years of being stingy, from ten years of making boots last another season, from two terms as sheriff in a helling cow town where a lawman's salary was high because few sheriffs ever lasted to collect their pay from the county. "I earned that money," Sargent said.

"How?"

Sargent pushed his back up against the wall. He could not see any better, but he could see well enough to know he had no chance to get clear by force. "That's my business. Why don't you come out in the light, or do you favor dark places . . . like alleys and such?"

"What did you want with Bledsoe?" The voice was patient.

"Personal business."

"There's an old prospect hole under this building, Sargent. I can't stay here too long myself, but you might stay a long time."

If there had been any threat or bluster, Sargent could have laughed, but he already knew, and the quiet voice confirmed that he was deep into a game where laughing was the sound of a fool.

"You came into town with a look in your eye, Sargent. You made talk with the hosteler who always took care of Bledsoe's horse. You made Marty Packard sore with your questions about Bledsoe. You went back to the hosteler's house for another talk about Bledsoe. And then the Golden Bear. That was Monte Bledsoe you scared out of the alley, just when he was walking into my arms. I don't feel kindly toward you, Sargent. You'd better talk."

"All right. Bledsoe maybe was involved in the killing of a friend of mine."

"Weaver?"

"No, I never heard of Weaver until today."

"Saddler?"

"The express agent?" Sargent said. "He's not dead."

"He died last night in Alder."

"I didn't know him." Sargent felt along the edge of the bed, under the mattress. There was nothing loose there.

"Who was the friend?"

"A man named Volpondo."

There was a long silence. In the other room the ringing of heavy metal went on monotonously.

"Pat Volpondo?" the voice asked.

"Uhn-huh."

"Did he have any other names?"

"José Enrique."

"Where was he from?"

"The Trinchera Ranch."

"Where did you know him?"

"We were raised together."

"Where?"

"The Double S, near Alder."

"Who owned it?"

"My uncle, Clay Sargent."

"What was Volpondo doing over in this country?"

"I didn't say he was over here, but he was," Sargent said. "We had some plans."

The man came around the chimney. He laid Sargent's pistol on the table beside the lamp and took the shield from the lamp.

He was a stocky man, dressed in blue-green tweeds. His face was full of sharp angles that contrasted oddly with the stockiness of his build. Sargent had seen him eating supper that evening with Marty Packard.

He said: "I made a mistake that couldn't be helped. Here's your loot on the table." He hesitated. "That freshly whetted knife doesn't seem to fit you, Sargent."

"The idea behind it fits." Sargent swung off the bunk. Pain flashed down from his skull and made the sides of his jaws and his neck ache. "Now, who the hell are you?"

"Mike Hanawalt."

Superintendent of the mountain division of Western Express, if it was true. "How do I know that?" Sargent asked.

The man took cards from a wallet. One of them bore a picture and descriptive data. Sargent made a slow check, word by word, feature by feature. One hundred and ninety pounds. Hair: dark red, streaked with gray. Eyes: green. Everything matched. Sargent gave the cards back.

"All right, you're Hanawalt. You knew my name."

"Hotel register. It didn't dawn on me for a long time that you were the fellow Volpondo planned to ranch with near

Weston. You came down an alley, scared Bledsoe away, wrecked one of my best men. I had to look you over. I'm sorry you got banged on the head in the deal." Hanawalt grinned. It was a full-grown expression of friendliness, but it came and went like a wink. Hanawalt pushed open the door to the other room. "Anything you want at the oven, Tom?"

A little man with fluffy side whiskers came to the door. He was wearing a derby hat, smoking a cigar, and the ashes of the cigar were spilling against a mortar and pestle in his hands. He went to the oven in the huge chimney and peered at a thermometer. "No hurry, Mike." He walked out without a glance at Sargent, closing the door as he went.

Assay shop, Sargent thought. He should have known before this.

"Sit down," Hanawalt said. "Would a drink of whiskey help your head any?"

"It can't hurt any. What did you use?"

"Blackjack." Hanawalt took a bottle from a shelf. "You got the best of it." He blew dust from two beakers. "I hope Tom didn't have sulphuric acid in these. You busted two of McClellan's fingers, dislocated his shoulder, and cracked three or four ribs. You ruined a good agent for me."

113

They sat at the table, drinking from the beakers.

"Tell me about Volpondo," Hanawalt said.

Sargent gave him the sharp facts.

Hanawalt shook his head. "Someone thought he was still working for Western." He stared bleakly at Sargent. "Pat was the best agent we ever had. On top of that, he was my friend." He poured another drink. "How'd you get onto Bledsoe's trail?"

"It looks like everyone has the same idea. Tallman mentioned the shooting. You trust Tallman?"

Hanawalt's eyes set quickly. "All the way. Why?"

"I wondered why he hadn't wired you about Pat."

"Maybe he did. I haven't been near my office for three days."

"How did Tallman know Pat had quit Western?"

"I told him that two or three weeks ago, when I was in Weston. You had the right idea, Sargent, when you took after Bledsoe. After the shooting here, that cleared the way to send the safe on to Weston. Bledsoe rode out of Turret. He went up on Fossil Ridge . . . that's about a half mile straight up from here . . . and he built a fire on the desert side of the range, a fine big fire."

"That let them know in Weston?"

Hanawalt nodded briskly. "That set up the Weston end of it, but how anyone knew the safe was loaded at Alder is another matter. There's two safes in an express car. One is bolted to the floor. That's for small valuables. The other safe we send back and forth, empty most of the time, to keep anyone from actually knowing when there's a payroll in it. We've had a little grief before on this run, Sargent, so we try to keep the enemy guessing." Hanawalt shook his head. "This time we handed it to 'em on a platter."

"How about the express messenger and the guard?"

"The guard didn't know. We sometimes send him along when the safe is empty. The messenger knew it was loaded, but only after it was in the car at Alder."

"You trust Wayne Hitchcock?"

"All the way," Hanawalt said. "Hitchcock got smashed up once at Costilla Pass, trying to protect a shipment when he should have let the thugs have it. We lost a guard in that one, too."

"How about the telegraphers?"

"Turret is a hot spot for gold, coming and

going. The telegrapher here is one of our own men." Hanawalt's smile winked on and off. "So's the relief operator. Nothing leaked down the wires, Sargent. Sure, after Hitchcock found out the agent here was wounded, he wired back to Alder. I told him to take the safe on to Burent in Weston, but, even if there was a leak from there on, it didn't help the robbers any. This deal was set up well in advance. The agent was shot an hour before the train pulled into here. The four men in Weston were as ready as rattlers, long before the safe started up the street with Hitchcock and Burent."

"Maybe you got leaks in the division office," Sargent said.

"I've thought of that, too. It would have to be me. I put the gold in the safe myself the night before. It was consigned to the Smuggler Mine."

"Maybe the platform crews and the teamsters noticed the difference in weight."

"Uhn-uh. When the safe hasn't gold in it, it's loaded with pig lead, right down to the same poundage, almost."

Sargent leaned back in his chair. "You've got a problem, Hanawalt."

"You too, Sargent. You'll never know who killed Pat Volpondo until this thing is unwound."

"I'm not much interested in the safe, Hanawalt."

"There's five thousand for finding it."

Sargent shook his head.

"You're like Pat. He took wages . . . high ones, all right . . . but he wouldn't take blood money. There's eight thousand dollars to his credit in the Alder bank. I put it there for him. Reward money. He wouldn't touch it."

"I want the man," Sargent said.

"There's five thousand for them, too."

"That's nice. I want one man."

Hanawalt glanced at the knife on the table. "Maybe it does fit." He started to pour another drink. Sargent shook his head.

Someone banged on the front door of the assay office. Tom told him to go away. The man kept banging. Sargent and Hanawalt sat in silence while Tom let the man in and gave him a ticket for a sack of samples.

"Probably country rock," the assayer muttered when the customer was gone.

"Where is this place, anyway?" Sargent asked.

Hanawalt pointed toward a heavily barred back door. "About twenty feet from where I hit you. It makes things convenient for watching the Golden Bear."

"You got all the girls over there watching

Ginger, and watching for Bledsoe?"

"Quite a few. How much did Lily get from you?"

"Fifty bucks."

"I'll see that you get it back."

"Is there another man watching the back stairs?"

Hanawalt nodded. "I'm afraid the bird is gun shy now, but we've got to watch."

"What were you going to do with Bledsoe . . . give him the prospect-hole-under-the-floor treatment?"

Hanawalt smiled. Sargent wished the expression would stay a little longer. It left a man wondering if he had seen a smile at all. "There's no hole," Hanawalt said. "I put on a good show, though, I think."

"I'm not so sure it was a show." He was quite sure when he saw Hanawalt's face harden. Hanawalt might use the tools of bluff, but he was not the bluffing kind.

"I want a hundred and ninety thousand dollars back," the Western official said. "I want everybody concerned, and particularly the man who killed Volpondo, to get what's coming to them. I'm working outside the law. I'm supposed to be in my office in Alder, but I may never go back there until I've rammed my way through this deal some way. You've got a stake in it, too, Sargent.

I want you to work for me."

"No."

"With me, then?"

"I don't give a damn about your safe, Hanawalt."

"Everything is tied to it. I'm not asking you to look for the safe. Play your own game. Pat always did. All I ask is that you keep in touch with me, through Tom or through the telegrapher at the station." Hanawalt's eyes narrowed as he studied Sargent. "It seems to me that Pat mentioned once that he had a friend who was a sheriff in Wyoming."

"I did two terms as sheriff in a county there."

"Did two terms?"

"I didn't like it."

"Fine! What's your first move?"

"I'm going back to Weston." Sargent could not see that his status had changed any, and yet he felt restricted by his agreement. "What about Packard?"

Hanawalt was looking at one of the beakers. His lids and eyes came up like trap springs. "What about him?"

"Has he helped you any?"

Hanawalt shook his head.

"Is he a friend of yours?"

"No."

"You trust him?"

"I haven't had occasion to distrust him."

"You don't trust him, do you?"

"I don't quite get you, Sargent, but I'll say this. You'd better ride wide around Marty Packard. He's tough meat."

"There's buzzard meat involved in this affair." Sargent touched the knife. "There's a friend of mine named Benny Paez. He's looking for Monte Bledsoe, too. If Benny comes up your alley, you won't hear him, like you did me."

"Paez, yes. We checked on Bledsoe's horse with Paez. I'll have a talk with him to prevent another mess like tonight."

Sargent began to gather up his possessions. As he was strapping on his money belt, Hanawalt said: "That's quite a pile to save, doing sheriff's work."

"Uhn-huh."

"Better use the front door," Hanawalt said.

Tom unlocked the door for Sargent. The brim of the assayer's derby hat and his side whiskers put his face in shadows when he was not directly in the light. His voice was expressionless when he said: "So long."

The door closed, and a bar fell into place. Sargent was on a dark back street with the mountain almost against him. The West

Fork of the Sweetwater was running close to his feet, snarling at trash, stinking with the odor of mill chemicals. There were only a few dim lights in buildings along this street.

From the main stem of Turret the uproar came as strongly as it had before. It had been almighty quiet in the assay office, Sargent realized. He began to feel his way back toward the main part of town. Tom's solemn parting hung in his mind.

Chapter Ten

The horse tracks wandered. One might have thought they were the marks of a loose animal, cropping grass here and there, drifting in the general direction of the blue spruce thickets where the Middle Fork headed, somewhere up on the Emigrants. But the shoes were badly worn. One of them was almost loose. Benny Paez had commented about the shoes of Bledsoe's red roan. So Sargent stayed with the trail, and presently he knew for certain that he was not following a range animal, for loose horses, moving idly, do not at intervals stand on ridges to check their back trail.

Sargent had not cut the sign by accident after leaving Turret at dawn. He had cast back and forth among the rocks and tiny aspen parks. His reasoning told him that Monte Bledsoe, returning as he did to Turret, must have a camp somewhere not too far from the town. The Emigrants were too rough for hurried crossing or even hiding. Prospectors were gouging at every ledge of the Emigrants in the vicinity of Turret.

Sargent stopped on a red-brown ridge to make his plans. Indian Summer sun and haze took the harshness from the lava plain and the sand on the Weston side, where men were digging for a hundred thousand dollars. Tallman probably had ridden in from there again, his eyes pouch-marked, his face puzzled.

It was the spruce thickets, high up under the gray planes of the mountains, where Sargent had business. He frowned at the country. If this horse with the worn shoes belonged to Bledsoe, and Bledsoe was up there somewhere in the trees, sneaking up on him on horseback was out of the question. Bledsoe was like a buck mule deer, taking to heavy cover before daylight.

Sargent found a patch of grass not far from the booming creek and picketed Windy. Close to the gelding's leg he cut the rope deep enough so it would break if Windy went against it in earnest. Since the night at the Lava House in Weston, Sargent had faced the knowledge that any trip he took might be his last.

Once in the timber, the horse with worn shoes had been directed purposefully. It was afternoon before Sargent, moving slowly all the time, came to a place where a man had camped the night before. The fire had been shielded by a ledge. Below that, the horse had been tied on a short rope to a tree, and it had rubbed hindquarters against another tree. The hairs caught in the rough bark scales were red roan.

Sargent examined the site carefully. It had been used several times. Bledsoe was like a wary old timber buck, all right. He left open space to one side of him, up toward the mountains, and never used the same lair twice in a row. The ashes of his fire were still full-blooming, not yet settled into flatness.

When the man had left camp, he had ridden eastward, staying just inside the timber. Sargent sat down and ate food he had secured from *Señora* Paez before daylight. Prior to leaving Turret he had told Benny a few facts that would keep Benny living longer, and from Paez he had learned something that helped him fill in a pattern.

"I found out las' night that Packard ordered Weaver and Bledsoe out of town thee first time they fought," Paez had said. "He gave them one day. The marshal ees one who ees proud that no one argues weeth heem. But Weaver and Bledsoe, they did not leave, and Packard said no more about eet. He ees not afraid, and so what changed hees mind, Brock-ee?"

Sargent had his ideas. He thought he would check them when he caught up with Bledsoe.

Down in the timber a twig cracked. Sargent went flat behind a rock, and then reached out to recover the tortilla he had been eating. He laid his pistol before him and waited.

There were no other sounds, until off to his left clothing brushed a tree to make a rasping noise that was checked quickly. One man, or two? Sargent picked up the pistol. It was a half hour before Whitey Fallon came into the camp site. He was holding a carbine at hip height. His red face was deadly grim. When he came across Sargent's tracks, he threw his head up quickly.

"Right there, Fallon. Drop the short gun."

Fallon's face went white and bitter. After a moment, while his eyes probed the rocks, he dropped his carbine. Sargent stood up.

"What are you looking for, Fallon?"

"I didn't think it was you."

"Bledsoe?"

"Maybe." Fallon walked over to the camp site and looked it over. "I think I followed a wrong track this time. I take a look at everything that comes into Triangle range from the Turret country. Who's Bledsoe?"

"A man."

"I could have guessed that." The little straggles of Fallon's left eyebrow pinched upward as he saw Sargent take a bite of tortilla. "We lost a lot of beef to Turret butcher shops. It got stopped. I don't want it starting again."

Sargent put his gun away. "We're even, Whitey. When did you first see this red roan's tracks?"

"You're a hell for the color of horses, ain't you? About four, five days back. It worried me. I couldn't take any time away from roundup until this morning."

"This fellow is playing for something bigger than a few steers," Sargent said.

Fallon picked up his carbine. "I'm about satisfied it ain't beef." He gave Sargent a long look, and it seemed that he was about to say something more, but he changed his mind and put the weight of his glance on Sargent.

"To make real sure, do you want to help me track the man down?" Sargent asked him.

Fallon shook his head. "If he ain't hurting Triangle, I don't care who he is."

It came to Sargent that Fallon was of the old school with a deep ranch loyalty that would keep him quiet about a good many things, if they did not rebound to the credit

126

of his employer and Triangle Y.

"You still say Pete Weston rode that gray gelding somewhere on this fork the day a man was killed?"

"I say it." Fallon's face was blank, set.

"You checked, didn't you . . . as far as you could?"

"Maybe."

He *had* checked. Fallon was worried. He would always worry about anything that might hurt Triangle. Sargent said: "Hitchcock's own son blew up on him after a quarrel."

Fallon's pale eyes grew dangerous. "Hitchcock regrets it, but he's a proud, stubborn man. He'll take him back, but he'll never ask him back . . . and he knows that Wayne will never try to patch up the quarrel."

"Did he take Pete Weston in as sort of a second son, old blundering, loud Pete? Fletcher Hitchcock must have been pretty good to Pete . . . to make him behave by merely raising a finger at him."

"Maybe," Fallon said. The hostility was gone, but he still did not care to discuss the matter with an outsider.

"And now," Sargent said, "with certain other worries that your boss has" — Fallon's eyes began to flare up again — "he's afraid that Pete might have been involved in the express robbery. That would just about break old Fletcher Hitchcock's heart."

The Triangle foreman stared.

Sargent laid it out slowly. "I think Hitchcock himself sent you out to check the gray's whereabouts on the day Pat Volpondo was killed."

Fallon's face did not seem to change, but Sargent was sure he had hit the truth.

"You're welcome to your ideas, Sargent." Fallon turned down the hill. "Just don't cause Triangle any trouble with them ideas."

Triangle first. To hell with anything else. It was understandable, and it was honest. Sargent felt a deep-down liking for Whitey Fallon. Fletcher Hitchcock was lucky to have a man like him around.

"If you happen to go by my horse, near where a little creek comes into the Fork from the west, will you see if he's snarled up?" Sargent asked.

Fallon raised one hand but did not speak or look back. Sargent turned once more to his tracking.

According to Paez, Monte Bledsoe was a close-mouthed man whose eyes never rested long in one place. His right ear lobe had been shot off. The last was enough, Paez had said, and the examination should be made after death.

Sargent had horse tracks to follow. The rest would depend on many factors. A buck that was afraid of pursuit would never stop long. It would range, circle back, keep moving after short rests. If pressed hard enough, it would at last crash completely out of the country. This buck would do everything but the last.

Keeping away from exposed points, Sargent climbed toward the gray sheets of rock above timber, and sat there an hour, studying the Middle Fork country. All the time he kept thinking that a buck deer would do this, and a buck deer would do that. Brock Sargent had trailed down bigger bucks than Bledsoe, horned and otherwise.

It was the second day after meeting Fallon. Sargent was out of grub. He had been down twice to check on Windy and to hang his saddle so the rats could not get at the sweet grease of the leather. He caught Bledsoe by using patience and a pattern the man himself had established, a nervous circling in the timber. He caught him in a place where Bledsoe had to lead his horse, where dead timber of a forgotten forest fire lay like toppled tombstones.

Fear was in Bledsoe. His face was haggard, rank with straight black whiskers. He came warily, trusting only the ground before him that he could see, trusting nothing behind him. On his right was a small cliff that ran for a hundred yards. Up the hill was a tangle of fallen timber, resting on rocks. There was a natural passage at the upper end of the cliff. Sargent commanded that, lying in the hole left by an uprooted tree, watching from between the roots. Bledsoe saw the way and did not trust it. He stopped, his eyes darting as he listened to the silent forest. The red roan was tired, dispirited. It probably had been close-tied without a chance to forage.

Bledsoe started toward the passage. He jerked savagely on the reins and cursed when the horse snapped a dead limb as its hind leg bent in crossing a log. Sargent let him come.

"Right there, Bledsoe. Hold it!"

Every nerve in the man's body must have snapped. His muscles tightened and made him shudder; and then he was stock still, with his eyes staring at the mass of tangled roots and earth.

Sargent was coming out of the hole when Bledsoe moved like a weasel. The man ducked under the neck of the horse, still clinging to the reins, reaching for his pistol. Sargent could have killed him, but he did not want him dead. Standing at the shoulder of the red roan, Bledsoe fired over the horse, a snap shot that grazed Sargent's side as he rolled back into the hole.

The horse tried to bolt. Bledsoe sawed its neck around and held it, and then he let it go at a trot, staying behind its shoulder. The front sight of Sargent's pistol was on the sprinkled red behind the animal's shoulder, and then he shook his head. There were six legs scissoring there before his gun. Sargent shot twice. The second bullet knocked one of Bledsoe's legs from under him. The red roan whirled sidewise and tried to pull away. Bledsoe still held it from the ground, but now he was exposed. He tried to rise. His wounded leg, the tugging of the horse pulled him down again. He sent two shots into the roots above Sargent's head.

With terror cracking in his voice, Bledsoe cursed. He emptied his gun. He tried to crawl to the horse. Sargent ran forward and jerked the reins from his hands, and stood looking down at him. He had been sure before, but now he saw the ear.

"Go ahead!" Bledsoe said. "Go ahead, damn you!"

His left leg was shattered just above the

ankle. It was not a pretty wound. Bledsoe did not look at it. He lay back against the hill, and his face said that he considered himself dead. Sargent jerked the saddle from the horse. The animal's back was sore from a wrinkled, dirty Navajo blanket. Sargent did what he could for Bledsoe's broken leg.

After a while the man's eyes steadied, and he seemed puzzled. Bledsoe asked: "Who are you?"

"I'm one of the bunch that handled the Weston end of it. I took care of Volpondo, the express company man."

"Volpondo?"

Bledsoe's face was bleak and gray with the shock of his wound. Sargent thought he could not have faked the question. "I'm another one of the bunch that was being crowded out of his end of the gold," Sargent lied. "I only wanted to talk to you, Bledsoe. You made it tough on yourself."

"How did I know? Day and night, I haven't had any sleep. I've been trailed. He tried to get me in Turret. A man's nerves can stand just so much. Give me a smoke, for Christ's sake. I been out of grub. I been. . . ." Bledsoe fainted.

Sargent looked at the wound again. The bullet had smashed the front of the leg, and bleeding was from surface veins only. He rolled a smoke and unslung his canteen. Looking at Bledsoe's pinched face, Sargent thought he could understand the man's terror. All of a hundred thousand dollars wasn't worth the days and nights Bledsoe had gone through. It was a harsh, dirty game, and Bledsoe had not been up to it.

The man's breathing began to level out, and presently he was conscious again. Sargent gave him a drink and lit the cigarette for him.

"You were one of the bunch from this side, huh?" he asked.

Sargent nodded.

"I never knew who any of them were. Four of you?"

"Five."

Bledsoe inhaled his smoke. "Somebody's going to get crowded."

"It shouldn't be me or you. Did Packard ever make any hints that way?"

"Not at first, not until after he told me to kill Weaver to make it look even better. Then I got to thinking. I could see that killing Weaver was not so much to make the fight look good as it was to make one less to split with. When I come back after the fight, I saw it in Packard's eyes. He figured to kill me right there in the Teamsters' Bar. I crawled. I had to. He couldn't do it then. Not even him. There was too many watching."

"You got back to Ginger once, didn't you?"

"Just once. Now I don't even trust her. Maybe she tipped Packard. Last time I was there, he had a man come up the alley after me." Bledsoe's darting eyes settled in suspicion. "How do you know about Ginger, if you worked this side of it?"

"I saw Packard a few days ago. You're right, Bledsoe. He wants all of us out of the way."

Bledsoe was still suspicious. "Where's the gold?"

"This side of the lava."

"You ain't already got clear with it?"

"Would I be here?" Sargent asked. "I got ten thousand of that coming." He studied Bledsoe keenly. "You had the easy part, just the shooting there in Turret and the signal fire that tipped us off over here. Who planned the whole thing anyway? Packard is the only one I ever dealt with."

Bledsoe tried to move his leg. He grimaced in pain, closing his eyes. "Another drink."

Sargent leaned over with the canteen. Bledsoe rolled his eyes. His left hand shot out suddenly like a striking snake. Sargent's gun was out of the holster before he got his hand on Bledsoe's wrist. The wounded man cupped his right hand around a rock at his side and cracked it against Sargent's head.

It was sharp and brief. Sargent's wrist was torn by the hammer of the gun, and he took another blow from the rock against his fending elbow before he chopped his right fist against Bledsoe's jaw. Even then the man did not go completely out, but he was helpless for a moment.

Sargent stepped back, returning his pistol to the holster. His left elbow was shooting pain both ways, and he could not bend the arm for several moments. *Where in hell have I bobbled after a perfect start?*

Bledsoe's eyes blinked back to awareness. His expression was sullen, bitter. "You slipped, brother," he said. "There wasn't any fire."

After all the lucky guesses to keep Bledsoe talking, mention of the signal fire had seemed to be a sure thing, straight from Mike Hanawalt. Nothing was sure in this game. One wrong word could get a man killed.

"You're caught," Sargent said. "You're marked for beefing anyway, by Packard, by the others. Tell me what I want to know and I'll take you in to a doctor and turn you scot-free, with an accident story to explain the wound."

Bledsoe's mouth was clamped.

"I'm telling the truth now." Sargent was, and it came easier.

It did not impress Bledsoe. He stared his hatred of Sargent and his hatred of himself for being trapped.

"The gold I don't care about, Bledsoe. I want the man who planned it all." Sargent was sure Bledsoe did not even know about Volpondo, and he was sure that Marty Packard did not carry enough above the shoulders to be the leader.

Bledsoe seemed to be considering. "Give me my gun back and let me ride away from here?"

Sargent nodded.

"Packard."

"Uhn-uh. You've got to do better than that."

"He's the one," Bledsoe said.

Sargent studied the man's face. There was not much to go on. Sargent made his decision. Bledsoe hated Packard and would lay the blame on him if he could, but Bledsoe did not know who had rigged the robbery.

"How was the signal sent from Turret that the safe was on the train?"

"I don't know, but there wasn't any fire."

I've caught small fry, Sargent thought, *but I've learned something. With patience and a lot of luck to keep breathing, I could get where I want to go.* With a small stick he jammed the chamber of Bledsoe's pistol, breaking the wood off against the steel. Bledsoe could work it loose, but it would take a little time.

Sargent checked the saddle on the red roan and was of a mind to let Bledsoe walk when he again looked at the horse's back. He led the animal to a high rock and said: "Hop it, crawl it, anyway you can make it."

Bledsoe made it, hopping on his good leg. He crawled up on the rock and rolled into the saddle. Sargent tossed up the reins, then he stepped back, and tossed up the pistol.

"Better head to Weston and get that leg fixed."

Bledsoe did not answer. He rode west, toward Turret. Sargent was convinced he was bought and paid for, if he went there. It would take a little time to get Windy and more time to get on Bledsoe's trail again.

Packard, no. He was taking orders. The man who had planned the robbery might be. . . . Sargent did not like the thought, but it was there.

Chapter Eleven

Two hours later Brock Sargent left Windy under a little hill and went up on foot to see how Bledsoe was doing. He was there ahead, moving slowly through the rocks, still headed for Turret. The red roan was dead tired, and Bledsoe was slumped over, holding to the horn with both hands. The horse labored up a steep pitch and stopped of its own accord, standing there with the dying sun on it. Bledsoe turned his head slowly to look behind him.

Flat and hard the rifle sounded. The red roan bunched in the middle, humping, its nose almost touching the ground. Bledsoe threw his good leg across the horse, pivoting in the saddle to slide off. The second shot bent his back across the leather, and then he slid down. At the same time the red roan's nose dipped toward the earth and crashed.

Sargent raced down the hill and had his carbine. There was still a little drift of smoke from the rocks a hundred yards up the hill from where the horse and man lay. Nothing else moved up there, just a dying wisp of smoke and warm red rocks catching the sunset glow.

Once more Sargent went down the hill. He worked around it and began to crawl in toward Bledsoe. The rifleman should come down to have a look. A half hour passed. Sargent scraped bunch grass with his belly, slid between rocks, and worked in so close he knew there was no doubt about Monte Bledsoe or the horse.

The sun touched the gray Emigrants. No one came. Sargent still used caution when he went in. Both horse and man were dead. The horse had dignity in death. It once had been a beautiful animal. The only pity Sargent had for the other death was that Monte Bledsoe once had been a human being.

Sargent went up in the rocks as carefully as if he knew the rifleman were still there. He found two .30-30 shells and tracks where the man had run low to gain his ambush point — and farther away the place where the fellow had leaped off his horse hastily and tied it to a scraggly aspen. The rider had stayed behind a ridge. His sign led down — toward Weston.

The days of searching and mulling over facts and guesses and the sign told Sargent that the killing had been premeditated but the meeting either accidental or unexpected. He covered Bledsoe with the man's own tarp. His last act before leaving was to remove the saddle from the horse.

Darkness caught Sargent before he had followed the trail two miles, for he had to move with caution. The horse was newly shod. It was heading straight toward Triangle after a wide detour east. It seemed significant that the rider often went out of his way to avoid narrow places between trees and rocks — where his mount might leave hair.

Catch dogs bayed Sargent into Triangle when the moon was high. Whitey Fallon and Pete Weston bellowed at them from the bunkhouse porch, and then light broke at the door of the main house. Fletcher Hitchcock came out and said: "Who is it, Whitey?"

Weston lit a yard lantern on a crossarm. He cursed under his breath when he saw who the visitor was.

Chuck Ozanne and two riders Sargent did not know came from the bunkhouse.

"Sargent," Ozanne said. "We busted up the poker game for him." But he did not go away.

"I'd like to talk to you, Mister Hitchcock," Sargent said.

Windy kicked a catch dog, sniffing at his heels. The dog yelped, then came back snarling. Fallon drove it away.

"He told you once you wasn't welcome here," Weston said.

Monica Hardin came from the house and stood beside her uncle. "It's Brock!" she said.

"He better Brock out of . . . ," Weston began.

"Pete, stop it." Hitchcock's voice was patient. It changed when he said to Sargent: "Well, get down and come on in. Have someone take care of his horse, Whitey."

"Maybe he won't be here long," Ozanne said.

"Thank you, Mister Hitchcock," Sargent said, dismounting. "Ozanne is right. Windy can stand."

Monica took Sargent's arm when he reached the porch. She ushered him inside. Hitchcock followed, his face gaunt and old in the light of a huge overhead lamp. The room was solid like the house, simple but with heavy furniture.

"I'll get you something to eat. I'll bet you haven't eaten for days, Brock." Monica smiled.

"Never mind, thanks."

"Get him something to eat!" Hitchcock

growled. There was no patience in his voice now. He did not care whether Sargent ate or not. He wanted Monica out of the room.

Monica released Sargent's arm. "Why, yes, Uncle Fletcher." Sargent watched the sway of her body as she left the room.

Sargent sat down in a leather chair by a dead fireplace. Hitchcock stood. "Well?" he said.

"At sunset today a man named Bledsoe was killed in the rocks. I figure it was maybe a mile west of the head of Cripple Creek. A horse with new shoes came straight from the place toward here."

"What kind of horse?"

"I saw only tracks."

"Toward here, not here, huh?"

"Just toward. Before dark caught me, the tracks were mixing in with other signs . . . new shoes again."

"Our whole corral was shoed the last few days," Hitchcock said, "and so was some of the stuff at Anchor. I never heard of a man named Bledsoe."

"He killed the express agent at Turret last week. Do you mind telling me who was out that way today?"

"Why don't you say, 'Which one of your men did it?' " Hitchcock asked savagely. It was not all anger with him; there was fear and worry, too.

Sargent sat with his hat on his knees and said nothing.

"I was up that way today, not as far as the head of Cripple Creek, but up there. I met Clum Brand and Carstairs, from Anchor. They were on their way back from the break down into the West Fork."

"These tracks led toward Triangle. Where was Pete?"

"What have you got against Pete?"

"Nothing, although he thinks I have."

"You insulted both him and Clum in The Crusher. You tried to make them look like blind fools, or else a pair of sneaky killers! I might just turn Pete loose on you, Sargent. You're making a lot of trouble around here."

"The trouble was already here, Mister Hitchcock." The words were soft, deliberate.

They cut into Hitchcock's anger, and his quick change of expression said they were true. "Pete was on the Middle Fork today, and so was Chuck. Whitey was over toward Theobold's cabins. Does that take care of you?"

"It would help," Sargent said, "if you would tell me why you think one of your men, maybe more, had a part in that robbery."

"Why, damn you, you whelp! This makes twice you've pushed your way . . . !"

"Not pushing, Mister Hitchcock. I want the same thing you want . . . the truth, only I'm not afraid of it. I lost the best friend I ever had in this mess . . . and he was not even concerned with it. If the man I want is Triangle, I can't help it, can I?"

"If I had a man in that dirty mess, I'd kill him as quick as you would, Sargent." The truth of his own words shocked Hitchcock. He stared at nothing for a moment.

He was mortally afraid that Pete Weston was the man, Sargent thought. *And maybe Pete was.* "Did Whitey tell you I was trailing this Bledsoe when I met him?"

"He mentioned it."

"I caught Bledsoe. He was guilty as hell in the safe robbery, but that was not why I wanted him. I turned him loose, hoping to trail him to someone who knew what I wanted to know. I wasn't more than three hundred yards behind him when he got shot. I don't care who hauled away the safe, Mister Hitchcock, but I want the man who killed my friend. He was tied to the stirrup of a heller stallion . . . and he was alive when that took place. I want that man, and

I don't care where he works."

There was sweat on Hitchcock's broad forehead, but he seemed relieved. "Pete wouldn't do a trick like that. Uhn-uh."

"I didn't size him up that way. I'm glad to hear you say it. Who would do it?"

Hitchcock blinked at the sudden sharpness of the question. "I don't know. I only know Pete wouldn't."

Monica came to the kitchen doorway. "Where's the hungry man?"

Hitchcock stared at her, then he looked at Sargent, and nodded toward the kitchen. *It was odd,* Sargent thought, *that there was no frippery in the room, with two women on the place.* Hitchcock stayed in the living room.

Mrs. Sommers, the gray-haired woman who must be the housekeeper, was in the kitchen with Monica. The older woman nodded at Sargent, then pointed toward a wash pan in a tin sink.

"You can run along, Missus Sommers," Monica said.

The look that Mrs. Sommers gave the younger woman did not carry any of the baffled quality of Hitchcock's expression when he was looking at Monica.

"Have you changed your mind about ranching here, Brock?" Monica asked as she sat down at the table with Sargent.

"No."

"Too bad. We need a new neighbor here."

"Ozanne wouldn't say so."

Monica smiled. Sargent had never seen a better-looking woman, or one who seemed more straightforward, but there were other facts that troubled him. *She needed handling. A man might straighten her out by. . . .* He gave up this line of thought when he saw her studying him as if she knew his mind. He began to eat.

"Chuck Ozanne," she said, and laughed.

Low enough so Hitchcock could not hear, Sargent said: "Wayne Hitchcock, too?"

It jarred her a little, but not much. "That was different," she said. "It was all on his side, the way it is with Ozanne . . . now."

I'd better stick to eating, Sargent thought. *No wonder Fletcher Hitchcock carried a baffled look.* Sargent did not dally long. Monica went with him when he left the ranch house. Hitchcock nodded as they went through the living room. He was standing at the mantel, tall, gray, gaunt.

In the yard Monica said: "Get those dogs out of the way, Whitey."

The dogs were lying at the foot of the pole that held the lantern crossarm. Sargent could not see Whitey, but after a few moments the foreman called from where he stood in darkness near a corral. The three big dogs got up and trotted toward him.

"When will you be back, Brock?"

Sargent swung up. The poker game was going its noisy way in the bunkhouse. At least one man besides Fallon had not resumed play. The red glow of a cigarette showed where the second man stood near the corner of the bunkhouse.

Sargent looked down at Monica. "I couldn't say. It might be quite a while."

Ozanne's voice came from the corner of the bunkhouse. "Make it longer, Sargent."

The woman gave no indication that she had heard. Sargent smiled at her. She might be putting a fine kink in affairs at Triangle, but he liked her. If he had any permanent interest in the country, he just might start something that would relieve old Fletcher Hitchcock of part of his worries. Hitchcock was judging Monica as he would a man. That wouldn't work.

She watched Sargent steadily. In the darkness near the corrals Fallon told the dogs to lie down. At the corner of the bunkhouse Ozanne flipped his cigarette away. Weston in the poker game laughed loudly at something. Through the windows of the main house Sargent saw Hitchcock, still standing at the mantel.

"Good night, Monica," Sargent said.

Windy went down the Middle Fork trail as if going home. Now and then, on crests, the lights of Weston showed. There seemed to be more life there than there had been when Sargent last looked on the town in darkness. Beyond Weston he saw a few faint flickers out toward the lava, campfires of those looking for the safe.

He passed the cañon where he and Morton had looked down. Out of the night, from the muttering river far below, came the thought that Ulysses Morton's dream, unrealized, might give him more satisfaction in the end than Sargent's mission if fulfilled. Vengeance, Alma Burent had called it.

He came into Weston by way of the railroad station. The telegrapher's office light made a dim blob that barely reached the rails. A herd was bedded between the chutes and the West Fork, and somewhere near the water a rider was singing sleepily. This was far apart from the trails he had ridden during the last few days. This was a normal, happy picture.

Clum Brand was squatted by a fire near the chutes, drinking coffee. Blankets were piled nearby on broken bales of hay. When

Brand heard Windy coming in behind him, he did not turn. He said: "Come in and have some java, Gin."

"Thanks," Sargent said. "I will."

Brand dropped the cup into the fire and spun around. His gun streaked up. His face was dark and tense. He saw who it was and put his pistol away.

"A man generally calls out," he said. "By God, you ain't got any manners at all, Sargent!"

"The light was on me. I knew you heard me coming for a hundred yards. I should have called out . . . yes."

"Yeah." Brand was still tight inside. "Well, have the coffee, anyway."

Brand pulled the thumping pot from the fire, retrieved the cup, and gave it to Sargent.

"Anchor herd?" Sargent asked, pouring coffee.

"Yeah."

"Off the benches on Cripple Creek?"

"Mostly. Why?"

"See anybody up that way who might have been riding about a mile west of the head of the creek . . . today?"

"Carstairs and me met Fletch Hitchcock but not nowhere as far up as the head of Cripple Creek. Why?"

"I found a dead man up that way, a fellow named Monte Bledsoe." Sargent could not read anything but wariness on Brand's dark face.

"You find 'em about as fast as they're beefed, don't you, Sargent?"

Sargent nodded. "Some of them. There are others that are on somebody's book. You know, Brand . . . about this robbery . . . I think somebody used several men, just used them. Now they're on that little list."

Brand's eyes glittered across the fire. He was hunkered down with his elbows on his knees. His hands had been clasped tightly, but now he unloosed them and let his left knee sink a little lower. "Is that a fact?" he said. "There's quite a batch of you guys in Weston tonight. Why don't you go over and throw a study on the rest of them?"

Sargent rose. "Thanks for the coffee . . . and the advice." Never again would he be careless around Clum Brand.

The courthouse was dark. In the express office Sargent saw men, sitting or standing everywhere. He put Windy on the dark side of the street and watched. Tallman was there, sitting on the counter beside a man with his right arm in a sling. That one, Sargent guessed, would be McClellan, the

150

agent he had thrown against the stair rail in Turret.

There were three others whom Sargent did not know. He did know Theobold, sitting on the desk, and Mike Hanawalt who was moving in the center of the floor, doing the talking. Sargent hesitated a few moments longer, and then he rode on over to the livery stable.

Morton came down from his living quarters as Sargent was lighting a lantern. He stopped with his face in the shadows, and his gloomy voice came softly. "I'm glad you made it back all right."

"Didn't you expect me to?"

"A man don't know. He just don't." Morton took the rig into the harness room, and then he helped rub down the gelding. "I found a couple of items the day I left you. Tallman's got them. He can tell you what I told him."

Sargent asked his question with his eyes.

"I'm sick of thinking about it," Morton said. "I got too deep into this trouble already. It's all over a pile of gold that won't do nobody any good, found or unfound."

"I'm not trying to find the gold, Morton."

"I know. Will it help him any . . . what you're doing?"

"It's in my mind that it will help me to

feel better." Sargent wondered if it would. "Do you mind if I pitch out under a wagon in your yard tonight?"

"Yes," Morton said. "You'll come upstairs and sleep in a decent bed. You look like you been laid out on rocks for a week."

At the water trough, while Windy drank, Sargent looked down the street. "Things have picked up a little."

"About half the men from Weston came back from digging in the desert," Morton said. He rubbed Windy's shoulder. "Sargent, I been wondering why you never said a word about getting shot at in the Lava House."

"Nothing to say. I couldn't even guess who did it. So why work my jaws?"

"You're an odd man, too serious, maybe," Morton said. "This Windy horse . . . he'll go to the stall without us, won't he?"

"Yeah."

"I want to show you something around back."

Sargent stumbled behind Morton into the wagon yard. They passed the dim hulks of high-wheelers, and then Morton put out his arm in warning and stopped Sargent suddenly. They stood in utter darkness.

"Smell it?" Morton asked.

"Smell what?"

"You can . . . after you know it." Morton lit a match.

They were almost against a tree, standing in a depression of reddish soil damp from water. Morton lit a lantern on the endgate of a wagon. "Now look at it!"

It was a peach tree, sturdy, flourishing, its leaves dark green in the lantern light. It was a moment before Sargent saw that the branches were loaded with fruit.

"What do you think of that, Sargent?"

"Fine."

Maybe there was not enough enthusiasm. Morton raised the lantern glass and blew out the light. "I can see it even in the dark," he said. "I can see the mesas there above the graveyard shining with rows and rows of trees like this." His voice ran slowly. "What can you see, Sargent . . . just a mound there on the hillside below?"

It was unreal, standing here in the darkness before a tree in a yard full of dying freight wagons, and still the picture of trees standing in green rows beside running water on the piñon mesas was sharp in Sargent's mind.

"You have something honest here, Morton."

That seemed to satisfy him. "I think so," he said. "Even if it never happens."

They returned to the building. Windy was crunching away in a stall. Morton tied the halter. They climbed the stairs with the scent of hay and the warm, fresh smells of a well-kept stable in their nostrils.

"I didn't know a peach tree had any scent unless it was in bloom," Sargent said.

"You got to know it. . . ."

Chapter Twelve

Hadley, the county clerk, moved briskly away from the closed door of Sheriff Tallman's office as Sargent entered the courthouse not long after breakfast the next morning. Sargent stood a moment before the door, looking at Hadley, who peered unabashed from his own office, wiping his white mustache with his hand. Someone was talking in Tallman's office, but the words did not come through the heavy oak. Still looking at Hadley, Sargent knocked on the door.

Mike Hanawalt had his feet on the window sill this time. Tallman was standing, just completing the buckling of his gun belt. Hanawalt's quick smile was on his face, then gone. "Well!" he said. "Another man for the expedition, Sheriff."

"I think I can handle things," Tallman said, but he appeared glad to see Sargent. "Any news?"

Sargent looked at Hanawalt. "Bledsoe is dead."

Hanawalt's features seemed to sharpen.

"I wanted that man alive."

"So did I," Sargent said. "I turned him loose to see who he'd run to in Turret. Somebody got him."

"Who?" Hanawalt asked.

Sargent shook his head.

Tallman sat down on his desk. "That's the man who killed Saddler, huh?"

"Did he talk?" Hanawalt asked.

Sargent said: "He knew what he did, that was all. By the way, Hanawalt, how did you know Bledsoe set the signal fire?"

"He didn't. That was our mistake. Timber cutters working for the Smuggler set that fire. I found out later. Bledsoe didn't know who was in on the robbery, did he?"

"No. What's new on the safe?" Sargent asked.

Tallman grunted. "That safe just ain't out there."

"Where is it, then?" Hanawalt asked quietly.

"This business in a few minutes may help us find out." Tallman went around his desk. He took a .45 pistol and a short length of frayed manila rope from a drawer. "That Colt saved my neck out in the Sodas three years ago. Morton found the pistol about a quarter of a mile from where Volpondo was. The rope had busted in the thicket, and rats had dragged it off into the rocks."

One butt grip of the Colt was broken and there was a bright gouge on the frame, and Sargent saw all over again the violence of the sorrel stallion's running through the rocks. He did not want to think about the rope at all.

From the floor behind his desk Tallman lifted several pieces of time-grayed oak with charred ends. "What would you say those are, Sargent?"

"One of them looks like the end of a shaft from a light spring wagon or buggy."

"Uhn-huh. They were part of the rack that carried the safe away. I brought them in from the lava two days ago. Should have the first time I saw them. They came, I think, from some old spring wagons in Morton's yard."

Sargent was watching Hanawalt. "What makes you think so?"

"Morton," Tallman said.

"Odd old character," Hanawalt observed. "He says he was standing in the dark last week beside a peach tree he's got in his wagon yard. He heard someone rattling around one of the wagons, so he followed the fellow when he left. He says it was a local cowboy . . . what was that name, Tallman?"

"Clum Brand."

"He's sure?" Sargent asked.

"If he wasn't damn' double sure, he wouldn't have said anything. I showed him one of the pieces. He wouldn't say they come from his wagons." Tallman shook his head. "But he showed me that two pairs of shafts were missing, and finally he admitted he knew who took them."

"He kept quiet a long time," Hanawalt said.

"I never spread it around how I figured the safe was carried away," Tallman said. "Right now, nobody but us, the robbers, and Morton know."

"When did Morton tell you?" Hanawalt asked.

Tallman hesitated. It was apparent to Sargent that the express official and the sheriff had talked it over, but Tallman had not revealed everything. "Early last evening," Tallman said.

Hanawalt's eyes set in a hard, questioning look.

Tallman said: "I like time to mull things over. Clum was with the herd not a half hour after the robbery. Whitey says he was there all the time. I trust Whitey. . . ."

"You can't trust anybody!" Hanawalt said. "We'd better bring both of them in, right now!"

"I'm still sheriff of this county. Whitey would stretch a point, if it had anything to do with Triangle, but he wouldn't plumb out and out lie on a deal like this. Four men rode away with the safe. Why'd they need a fifth one in on it?"

"Let's get Brand and find out." Hanawalt stood up. Sargent saw the pistol in his left coat pocket.

"I'll handle it," Tallman said. "Brand's jumpy, always was. If strangers go crowding in on him, no telling what he'll do. I know Clum pretty well, and so. . . ."

"I'm going," Hanawalt said.

"No." Tallman shook his head gently.

Hanawalt reached inside his coat. "I'm a U. S. deputy marshal, Tallman. I have been, since the last robbery at Costilla Pass." He held a folded sheet of paper toward Tallman.

The sheriff read it, gave it back. He glanced at Sargent. "All right. All three of us. I'll do the talking."

Hadley chewed at his mustache as he watched them go down the hall.

They walked side by side across the baked yard of the courthouse. "Had a good stand of grass here once," Tallman muttered absently. Their boots swished into the sandy street. Sargent heard the rattle of a pump and looked over his shoulder. Alma Burent was at her well. She glanced at the three men, turned away, and then looked again quickly, caught by the intensity of their movements.

"Slow it down," Tallman said. "We look like we're carrying a hang rope. Talk a little. Damn it, I don't want to go in on Clum and rattle him."

"We'll let him do the talking later," Hanawalt said.

Hadley was walking rapidly across the courthouse yard, and then he broke into a run, headed for the main part of town.

The herd was grazing along the banks of the West Fork, held by two riders. A rawhide rope of a man with one tooth in the front part of his mouth was sitting on a bale of hay at the camp, trying to drive down a tack in his boot with the butt of a pistol. He read something in the manner of the three approaching men, and put on the boot quickly.

"Morning, Gin," Tallman said.

"You've got a man named Brand . . . ?" Hanawalt said.

"I'll handle it." Tallman looked at Hanawalt. "Get it in your head now."

Gin put his foot on the bale of hay and tugged at his boot. *Carstairs,* Sargent thought. *He looks as if he could be rough with that pistol.*

"Tell Clum I want to see him, will you, Gin?" Tallman asked.

Carstairs merely glanced at the sheriff. Acceptance, understanding was there. It was different when Carstairs sized up Sargent and Hanawalt. *Yes, he could be rough,* Sargent thought.

The lean Anchor boss nodded. He walked to his horse and rode away without hurry.

"Suppose he tells Brand to light out?" Hanawalt asked.

Tallman said nothing. He glanced at Sargent.

Carstairs rode to the man on the downstream side of the cattle. Then the two of them went around the herd to the other rider. Sargent understood. The upstream rider was Brand, between the herd and the hills, where the cattle would head if they got a chance. Carstairs was merely replacing Brand at a weak point. Sargent understood, but he did not like it. It meant that Carstairs expected something to scare the herd.

"Now all three of them are ready," Hanawalt said. "Why didn't we go out and get Brand?"

"Why don't you sit down on that bale of hay and rest yourself?" Tallman said.

Brand and Carstairs came in together. Twenty feet from camp they dismounted and walked, coming in at an angle, leaving the horses to one side of a possible trouble lane. Sargent shifted ground. He kept one eye on Carstairs.

"Yeah?" Brand looked at Tallman.

"You carried some shafts away from Morton's wagon yard, Clum." Tallman's voice was easy.

Brand's mouth twitched, and then his face was frozen quiet. "Who says I did?"

"You were seen, Clum."

"By who?"

"That don't matter," Tallman said. He was firm, but not digging or pushing. Sargent appreciated his strength. "I'd sort of like to know what for you took them shafts."

"Firewood."

"Hellsfire!" Hanawalt said. "Look, Tallman. . . ."

"Shut up," the sheriff said. He glanced at a pile of piñon wood. "Morton always hauls you boys plenty of fuel every year. Why'd you want those oak shafts, Clum?"

Brand was trapped, and he had known it

from the moment he had said one word too quickly. It showed in the darkening of his eyes, the whitening of his face under the black whiskers. He hung fire for an instant, and Sargent watched Gin Carstairs, ready to step in against Carstairs and grab his arms.

Carstairs was standing easy, so easy that he could move in a streak if he chose to. His lips were back, and his one front tooth stood like a forlorn brown stump. He was watching Brand.

There is a moment when violence holds its breath, and then it either explodes or moves away. Sargent took a glance at Brand, and there the moment was, and it was in Morse Tallman's voice as he said quietly: "Whitey Fallon says you were here the night of the robbery, Clum. I'll have to sort of hold you until I can talk to Whitey again."

"Sort of hold him!" Hanawalt said. "You're going to arrest him, Tallman . . . or I will!"

"Will you shut up!" Tallman, too, had seen the point of trouble stand still, and then start to move on, and his voice threw rage at Hanawalt. "Will you go with me, Clum?"

Sargent saw it run on Brand's face. Things were not too bad. They did not know too much. Brand opened his mouth. He started to nod.

From up the street there came the sound of loud voices. Men were coming hard, toward the chutes. *Hadley's big mouth had done a fine job,* Sargent thought angrily.

"That's a mob, Tallman!" Brand cried. "That's a hanging mob!"

"No, it ain't, Clum." Tallman's voice was still controlled.

"They ain't going to rough me up!" Brand went back a step. His hand went down to his pistol grip, but he was looking at the running men, not those before him.

"No, Clum, they. . . ."

The pistol shot shattered everything. Brand hunched his shoulders and squinted his eyes, and then he put his face against his chest and doubled over to the ground, turning sidewise as he fell.

Hanawalt's sharp face was white. His left hand was still in the pocket of his blue-green tweed coat, and smoke was drifting foully from the torn cloth.

"You damned fool!" Tallman said.

Gin Carstairs gave Hanawalt a bitter look, and then he knelt by Brand.

"He started to draw!" Hanawalt said.

"He didn't, not against us," Tallman said. "He would have gone with me."

The running men swarmed in on the scene. Hadley was one of the first. "Got one of the robbers, huh? I see you got him, Sheriff. By God, you got him!"

Sargent took Hadley by the shirt collar and seat of the pants and threw him toward town. Hadley seemed more surprised than angry, and he was still around when they started to carry Clum Brand up the street in a tarpaulin. Brand died in the lobby of the Lava House while Theobold was getting the doctor out of bed.

Chapter Thirteen

Dr. Alton Cobb came to the loft of Morton's livery stable to see Sargent that evening. Cobb was not a drinking man and not a physical wreck. He had come to the edge of the lava to cure his tuberculosis some years before, and now he was well and intended to stay in Weston. He talked about the town, the climate, and the evils of drinking hard liquor all the time he poked and squinted at the bullet gash on Sargent's side. It wasn't anything, Sargent said, that little streak of broken skin where Monte Bledsoe's bullet had passed.

"Yes, it is," Cobb said. "It's a lucky thing Morton told me about your fever and that lump under your arm. Doggone seldom in this clean, dry climate we're bothered much by infections in bullet wounds, but you got one now. The wound's fine, but you got it in your blood, Sargent. You're going to be right here in bed for several days. You a drinking man?"

"Not much."

"That's good." Cobb smiled. "Maybe you'll live."

"I've been hit worse than this . . . without any infection." Sargent stood up. He felt the fever heat in his face, and he felt the dragging of it inside him, and he could not hold his arm against his body. He sat down on the bed.

"I'll send up some medicine," Cobb said. "It won't help, but I'm supposed to dish it out. Nice mess down there at the railroad today, wasn't it?"

"It was." Sargent rolled over on his back. Morton was at a work bench near a dormer window that looked out on the wagon yard and the peach tree. Shelves along the wall were filled with miniature stagecoaches and wagons carved from cedar, oak, and aspen. There must have been fifty. Dust was heavy on some of them. Morton was working on another.

"Keep him down, Ulysses," Cobb said. He put his thermometer in his bag and went down the stairs, whistling "Susanna."

"Is that his favorite song?" Sargent's mouth and tongue did not seem to function right.

"He whistles everything."

"Does he ride?"

"Buggy. He ain't much for saddle going." Morton came over to the bed. He was carving a stagecoach baggage rack from cedar, all in one piece. His knife dripped red and white shavings. He did not look at Sargent. "I didn't aim for Clum to get killed."

"Nobody did, not even Hanawalt. Hanawalt was scared. He's a dandy in a dark alley, but he was scared down there today." Afraid — but perhaps not in the way Sargent's words made it sound.

Morton nodded gloomily. "I got some medicine that'll help your fever, better'n anything Doc can throw together. I'll leave it with some water here on a chair by the bed. I got to help Alma clean up the old Briscoe eating house. I promised. She's going to start the place up in a day or two."

"Good for her."

"Theobold's putting up the money."

"I thought he was broke," Sargent said.

"It don't take much. He gets a little from his folks back East." Morton put the piece of wood and the tiny razored knife on his work bench near the dormer. "Something's kind of stirred Theobold up lately."

"What?"

"I don't know. He stirs, every now and then."

Alone, Sargent stared at sunset fire on the Sodas. He did not feel like moving, but his mind raced over a dozen things he should be doing, men he should be talking to, places he should be riding to if he were going to get his job done.

He moved restlessly. He sat up and gulped half the medicine Morton had left on a chair. It was brown and sticky and vile and three glasses of lukewarm water did not remove the taste. Sargent lay back against the dry hotness of his pillow.

The sun died, and the Sodas went lifeless, gathering gray to themselves. For a while the brown lava plain held a warm color, and then the dusk crept over it. Sargent listened to his own breathing. It was short and shallow. A miserable little scratch across his side . . . ! He moved his head to the other end of the pillow, and at once the heat was there. It was almost dark when he went to sleep.

The creaking of a chair roused him.

"Awake?" a man asked softly.

Sargent recognized Theobold's voice at once, but not until he sat up in utter darkness did he remember time in its place, and where he was.

"I brought the doctor's medicine . . . Cobb's Elixir of West Fork," Theobold said. "I saw no need to wake you. How do you feel?"

"Fine," Sargent said, still trying groggily

to adjust himself to the situation. "Light a lamp, will you?"

Theobold went across the room with sureness. While a lamp chimney was rattling on metal, he said: "Hanawalt left on the train tonight. I think Tallman urged him a little."

The strong, blunt bone structure of Theobold's face sprang out of the dark, and the light illumined a bronze tint on the thick tufts of his short-cropped hair. "You're as red as a spanked baby," he said. "Here, let me get you some fresh water."

He brought it from the bucket, and it was as warm as the water in the pitcher on the chair.

Sargent looked at Cobb's medicine. Green. He did not like the color, so he drank the rest of the brown mixture. Theobold picked up the bottle afterward, frowning. He smelled it. "Good Lord! That's what Morton uses on horses!"

Sargent was still drinking water, rubbing at the fuzz in his mouth with his tongue. "I'll bet he never got two doses down the same horse . . . if it lived past the first one." Sargent lay down again. "So Hanawalt sloped?"

"Uhn-huh." Theobald sat down. He was wearing black broadcloth again. His face was as firm and clean-shaven as the first time Sargent ever saw him. He looked at the sick man thoughtfully. "Figuring on another funeral? Too many men have died over a box of gold already."

Even through his fever it struck Sargent that there was an obscure meaning behind the words, as if Theobold had implied that he knew a way to clear up the affair.

"Morton says that gold is an evil, in itself." Theobold frowned. "Did he ever show you his peach tree, Sargent?"

"He did."

"Tell you about the dam?"

"He showed me the place."

"What did you think?"

"That he has an honest, worthwhile idea."

"So did I," Theobold said. "I've been wondering lately why I haven't done something to help him. You know what you did, Sargent, the day you came upon the hotel roof? You insulted me. You might just as well have said, 'What is the matter with you, sitting here in the middle of decay, just sitting?' Others have said it out loud. You said it with your attitude, and it hit me like a club. A man should be insulted once in a while, Sargent." Theobold smiled. "You got any money?"

"Not much. Why?"

"You were going to ranch. You know what I would have wanted to relinquish everything I hold on the East Fork? Ten thousand. Got that much, Sargent?"

"We might have raised it."

"Oh, yes, I forgot. The man you brought in that day. . . ." Theobold studied the carvings on the shelves. "Ulysses is a craftsman. Did you ever see anything so beautiful as those little coaches?"

"They're good."

"He's spent hours doing that in the last five years. He hates it. One day I saw him stop right in the middle of his carving and stare out the window at his peach tree. Then he carefully piled every miniature wagon on the floor. Very deliberately, he jumped up and down on them until there wasn't a whole piece in the entire room. It didn't help. There was no anger in it. I helped him clean up the mess, and then we got two bottles and started in. That helped. Morton loosened up then and began to talk. By morning, when we both were sitting against a wagon box outside, he was all right."

Theobold was silent for so long that Sargent rolled over on his elbow and looked at him, puzzled.

"A man builds something if he wants to

save himself," Theobold said. "That carving is fine, but not enough. I built the Lava House, started a ranch, started with Morton to build mines out in the Sodas. It all blew up, and I told myself it was too much. It wasn't enough. You build something all your life, Sargent, or you're no good. I spoke of physical things, but there are other ways to build, too."

Theobold leaned forward, his hands on his knees, his blunt face deadly serious. Then he leaned back in his chair and patted the arms, smiling. "I could preach before I could talk." He laughed gently. "Put it this way. You're the first sucker that's been around in a long time, the first man who might have a few thousand that Morton has been able to get near the dam site in years. What do you think of that peach-growing enterprise, Sargent?"

"It's all right. I'm not interested, that's all. I've got other business in Weston County."

"And then?"

"I'll leave."

"And then?" Theobold incised softly.

Sargent had not looked that far ahead. He tried to now, briefly, and all he saw was returning to Wyoming, and beyond that . . . ? It was none of Theobold's business, anyway. He rolled over on his pillow, staring at the ceiling.

"Vengeance builds nothing, Sargent."

"It's enough for me, right now. You must have been talking to Alma Burent."

"I did. In a way it was her idea that I give you the boring lecture that I just finished. She has tried to stir me out of my lethargy on occasion, without much luck. I find it easier to point out to others the errors of their ways."

"What's her interest in me?"

"More likely her interest is in helping Morton, if she can. You see, she sympathizes with his dream." Theobold stood up. "You should be resting. Is there anything you want?"

"I guess not. Thanks."

Theobold went down and returned with a bucket of water. He refilled the pitcher, blew out the lamp, and started to leave again. At the top of the stairs he stopped. "Wayne Hitchcock is the temporary express agent here now. Hanawalt sent him in tonight. That's the news, except that the gold is still unfound. Good night."

Again Sargent thought he sensed some obscure intention behind Theobold's words. Through a growing mist of fever he tried to close in on the idea, but all that he could see clearly was Monica Hardin, smiling at him, and at times he thought he felt the pressure of her fingers on his arm.

For two days her face came and went, and there were others that he could not see clearly, and there were muttering voices that enraged him because they did not speak so that he could understand. It lasted thirty-six hours. Theobold was sitting beside him when he woke, sweat-soaked, clear-headed. Theobold forced him into one of Morton's long-tailed night shirts, changed the blankets, and covered Sargent like a child.

Theobold went softly down the steps.

Sargent slept again, restfully, with tiny wakenings just long enough to remind him that normal sleep was wonderful. When he came out of that, the sun on the Sodas told him that it must be mid-morning of a day that he could count as having lived. Two men were with him then, Morton and Boley Adams, owner of The Crusher Saloon.

Morton grinned. "You'll be fine now. My medicine did it."

"Horse medicine."

"No difference. What do you want?"

"Grub," Sargent said.

"You mentioned something that's available," Morton said, and left promptly.

Sargent had forgotten how hoarse Boley's

voice was until the little saloonman said: "You really had something. Everybody knows it, except Pete and Ozanne. I kept telling them, 'Go see him, if you don't think so.' "

"What's the matter with them?"

Boley looked at the stagecoaches. "They think you been dogging it. They say you're scared to meet any of Brand's friends, after what happened at the railroad. Doc Cobb cussed 'em out and told 'em they was nuts, but they still keep saying you run away and went to bed."

"I didn't kill Brand."

"You might as well have, for all of Pete and Chuck."

"Are they sore at Tallman?"

"They don't say so, if they are." Boley spun his hat on his forefinger, and then he clapped it on his head. "Doc said you'd be out of it today. I thought you might go wandering out and run smack into Pete and Chuck before you had your strength back. Roundup's over. They're just hanging around town, drinking some."

Boley went to the stairs. "You don't know who told you." He removed his hat and spun it again. "That Pete . . . he can butt like a billy goat, Sargent. Just for fun, he's butted guys all over my place, busted chairs and tables. I got to be getting back."

"Thanks."

"Don't mention it. That's what I mean."

A little later Morton came in with a tray of food, covered with a white napkin. "Right from the Desert Cafe! Alma's doing real good. All the railroaders eat there. Theobold told 'em they couldn't cook in their rooms no more. Doc Cobb, he eats with Alma. Tallman, Hadley . . . she ain't doing bad at all. I was the cook for a while, but she finally got Missus Dunstan."

Morton threw the green medicine out of the window, and put the tray on the chair beside the bed. "Now, I said a big steak was the thing, but those women sort of cut me down to some soup and stuff."

Sargent ate everything in sight. He said: "I heard Weston and Ozanne have got an idea about me."

"They been drinking, talking too much. Weston never was too smart, but I never figured him thick enough to hold with a story like they're trying to spread."

"Were they really close friends of Brand's?"

"Yeah, they were. Brand worked at Triangle for a long time. He and Ozanne were real thick, until they got into a squabble over that woman at Triangle. Brand went over to Anchor. They patched things up afterward, though."

Sargent was trying to pick up the strands of thought that had been twisted and or unraveled by his fever. Those days he would never remember had changed him. What had been a compelling drive, a mission, was now an unpleasant task that should be finished. Before he had been moving intensely, with a cold patience directing every thought. Now, he wanted to get it over quickly. Habits of a lifetime told him that quickness often led to fatal error.

He was not thinking of Ozanne and Pete Wilson when he asked: "Has Tallman turned up anything new?"

"Fallon admitted that Brand might have been away from the herd the night of the robbery . . . maybe even a half hour. The cattle were dead quiet. Whitey says he fell asleep in the saddle for a while." Morton walked over to the window. "I wish I'd never told about Clum and those shafts."

There were Hadleys. There were Mortons. "Something doesn't stack up right," Sargent said. "I don't see why four men needed Brand at all. If four men couldn't handle seven hundred pounds . . . ?"

"Pete Weston could lift that much by himself." Morton turned around quickly. "I

178

don't mean nothing by that. I was just thinking maybe you ought to duck him some way for a while, anyway till Ozanne quits prodding him."

Boley had not mentioned that last. Ozanne, sure, working on big Pete, who liked to butt with his head and fight with other men, probably half from natural orneriness and half for sheer fun.

"Who took a few shots at me in the Lava House?" Sargent asked casually.

Morton's eyes widened. "I wouldn't even guess. We were talking about you sort of sliding away from Pete."

Sargent shook his head, his fever-blistered lips moving in a slow smile. "It won't work, Morton. Sooner or later I've got to step up and bust my hands on Weston and get knocked pizzle-end up. Then he'll be satisfied. If I was John L. and licked Pete, I think he'd still be satisfied." But perhaps Chuck Ozanne would not. Monica's flirting with Sargent might not be all the reason, either. It just might not be.

Sargent sat on the edge of the bed. He felt fine. He stood up, and that was different, but the sooner he was able to go downstairs, the better. He walked over toward the window. "Hey! What happened to the coaches?"

Morton's forehead began to redden. "I took some. . . ."

Someone rapped on the bottom step in the stable. "Hello up there! Anybody home?" It was Monica Hardin.

"That woman," Morton said. "Get back in bed!"

"I don't want her to see me that way."

"All right. Stand there with that night shirt rubbing your hairy knees, then." Morton went over to the head of the steps. "Come up, lady . . . miss."

A man could say the same every time, Sargent thought: *She was a downright clean-cut pretty woman, and not in her features only. She brought something bright and surging with her.* He got back in bed.

For a flashing tick of time the past snapped aside a curtain on a picture, a memory that Sargent thought he had forgotten. He had ridden through summer brightness to Trinchera to see Pat Volpondo after a year of being away. Standing in tall grass on the banks of Cutter Creek was the most beautiful sorrel mare he had ever seen, and he had said so. Pat had given him an odd, sad look and said: "She'll move in a minute."

The mare had moved. Both forelegs were malformed so terribly that it had twisted

180

Sargent's heart to watch.

And now, covered to the neck in a hot room, he felt some of the chill that had ridden back with that long-ago scene. Then Monica came over and put her hand on his forehead and kept smiling at him until the chill was gone.

"You've had a bad time, Brock."

"I got to see Boley," Morton muttered, and was gone.

Monica sat down on the edge of the bed. "You look awful, Brock. You're thin." She pressed her palms against his cheeks.

"I need a shave."

"You don't know how I've worried . . . just being up there, thinking." She put one hand across his body and leaned down.

He threw his arms clear of the covers. She strained against him, and they kissed as if the act had been long denied. Sargent's left hand was tight against the long muscle ridges of her back, the other clutching the soft mass of her hair.

For a long time elemental fierceness surged between them. It was still with Sargent when Monica pushed away, and rose. She stood there, smiling, her elbows hard back as she smoothed her hair. It was a pose designed for other purposes, and that was all right with Sargent, too.

"You can lick Pete Weston, can't you, Brock?"

"I doubt it."

"You could shoot him."

He doubted her seriousness. "Pete is not a pistol fighter, Monica. Come back here!"

"After all, this is a stable, Brock." She wrinkled her nose at him. "No, I've got to go now. I'm staying with Missus Dunstan a few days. Since there's a place to eat here, a person doesn't mind Weston so much."

Sargent held out his hand. "Come back . . . just once."

"You know where Missus Dunstan lives, don't you?" Her lithe walk took her across the room. She wrinkled her nose at him from the top of the stairs.

Sargent listened to her footsteps all the way. The sounds on wood stopped; she was crossing the stable, going toward the wide doors, out into sunshine. He swung out of bed. He had been here long enough. He looked around the room. Where the devil were his clothes?

Monica's voice came sharply. "Pete! What have you done now?"

Weston's voice was sheepish. "Well, the old cuss got in the way, and. . . ."

"You're an ox and a fool!" Monica said. "And you, Chuck . . . !"

"Going up to a man's room. Who's a fool? I've had about enough of your fancy prancing, Monica." Ozanne was about half drunk.

Sargent found his clothes lying on a camel-backed trunk behind some cedar boards. He was fighting into his Levi's when he heard the slap and heard Ozanne laugh.

"You haven't any business here!" Monica said.

"Speak for yourself, Monica. Come on, Pete, let's go up and drag the faker out."

"Damn' right!" Weston said. "Get out of here, Monica."

Sargent slammed leather through his belt buckle. He could not find his pistol. His hands were trembling as he grabbed clothing from the trunk. He knew he was not afraid; and he knew he did not have strength enough to lick a chipmunk. In a cobweb nest behind the trunk he saw an old Sharps rifle. He grabbed it and threw the block down. The chamber was empty.

Heavy weight beat against the bottom steps. Sargent went back to the bed and sat down, with the rifle across his knee. He could not hold it steadily any other way.

Sheriff Tallman's voice was a drawl, but it cut like a knife. "That's far enough, Pete. You too, Ozanne. Come on out here."

After a moment the heavy weight went

down the steps again.

"Butting in again, eh, Tallman?" The viciousness in Ozanne's voice was thick. "First, Clum, and now. . . ."

"That's enough, Chuck. Pete, I know you love to knock a man around, but this is the first time I ever saw you going after a sick man."

"He ain't sick," Weston growled.

"Pete, you're going crazy on whiskey," Monica said. "I'm going to tell Uncle Fletcher about this."

"I could tell him plenty about. . . ."

The slap sound came again. Without seeing any of it, Sargent pictured the scene as the actions of angry children, but he could guess how deep the involvements really were.

"Get across the street, Ozanne," Tallman said. "Pete, since you were busting to get up those steps, you just carry Morton up there."

Morton's voice came weakly. "No need of that."

"All right then, Pete. Go find that driller in Turret that you didn't have no luck with, if you got to fight." There was no anger in Tallman's voice.

"Big . . . with that pistol, ain't you?" Weston growled.

"The star, too. You didn't see neither one of them move, did you? Go on, Pete."

Ozanne said: "Monica, wait! I didn't mean . . . wait a minute, Monica!" His voice faded away from the building.

Tallman and Morton came up together. The corner of Morton's mouth was bleeding, and his face was white. He said nothing as he walked to the window and stared out. He was not a fighting man, probably never had been. He had tried to stop Weston and Ozanne there near the stable doors, and it might be that the result was the first time a man had ever laid hands on Ulysses Morton in anger. A thing like that hurt a man badly, Sargent knew.

Tallman took the Sharps. Before he set it in the corner behind the trunk, he flipped the block down and grunted. From a bureau drawer he took Sargent's gun belt and brought it to him. "Your other loot is in that drawer, too. Now get back in bed."

Sargent obeyed. The way he felt, it was only common sense to obey. The sheriff sat down and ran his hand across his eyes. "I never had no trouble handling Pete before, even in the middle of his hell-raising."

It did not seem to Sargent that Tallman had had much trouble this time.

At the window Morton reached up and

took a varnished Wells Fargo coach from a shelf. He looked at it a moment, then carefully set it on the floor, and put both feet on it. He stood there, twisting his boots, and then he went across the room and began to wash the blood from his face.

Tallman said: "Hanawalt's out on the lava with three, four men. Saw him this morning. Said he was sorry he lost his nerve the other day." He shook his head. "I still say that safe ain't out there. It's somewhere else, with the gold still inside."

Morton dried his face. He took two coaches from a shelf and went out.

"That bull-brained Pete Weston," Tallman said.

"Fletcher Hitchcock thinks a heap of him."

"When this place was booming, Pete was just a kid, big as he is now. He was always in trouble. One day a bunch started to hang him. I wasn't sheriff, then. Old Fletch had just kicked Wayne out a few months before. Fletch went in on that bunch, over in Mort's wagon yard. He clubbed a few, and rode his horse over a couple more. Fallon was with him. Fallon would go to hell with Fletch Hitchcock. They took Pete away from the mob. He's been at Triangle ever since. Fletch can cock an eye and stop Pete from doing anything."

"Trying to replace his son, eh?"

"I guess so," Tallman said. "If a thing like that can be done."

"Monica Hardin . . . ?" Sargent began to grope.

Tallman's loose-fleshed face held an odd look, the expression of a man trying to hide all expression. "She's the niece of Fletch's dead wife. Ulysses Morton and Alice Ashley were going to marry up one time, but something happened, and Fletch got the inside track. When Alice was dying, Fletch promised he'd take care of Monica. He's done his best. He's tried double hard since his own son and him busted up." The sheriff went to the window. "Morton told me once that tree reminds him of Alice. It's odd, but I know what he means." For a long time Tallman said nothing. Then he straightened his shoulders. "Well, nothing is settled. You still want a man. Western wants several . . . and a box of gold, and, since I'm a lawman, I got to want the same things."

"Marty Packard was in it," Sargent said. Tallman swung around. "Bledsoe spilled it."

"You didn't mention that to Hanawalt, Sargent."

"I saw him at a table with Packard at the Swampscott in Turret. Maybe that was nothing, but later Hanawalt warned me to circle Packard. I don't know just what he had in mind." Sargent told what Paez and Bledsoe had said about Packard. "You don't talk too freely to Hanawalt, either, Sheriff."

"Not often to anyone." Tallman paced the room slowly. "Packard told Bledsoe to kill Weaver, so that means Packard was in on the plan from the first, not making a shrewd guess and horning in after the Turret express agent was wounded. I don't hand Packard the brains to be the boss robber, but, if he wasn't, why was he needed at all?"

Sargent said: "When I hear from Paez, maybe we'll have an idea." He sat up suddenly. He put his words together slowly. "We've been figuring that only Wayne Hitchcock and Hanawalt knew the gold was on the train. The guard in the express car claims that Hitchcock never opened the door, never did anything that could have been a signal, all the way from Alder. Hanawalt says no wires about the shipment went through until after Hitchcock reached Turret. Saddler was shot an hour before that, so somebody knew."

"Yeah," Tallman said. "We know that."

"Somebody at the Smuggler Mine, maybe the superintendent, knew the payroll was coming. Maybe a code wire several days before. Packard hob-nobs with those mining men. One of them dropped it, Tallman. Packard had lots of time to make arrangements. Maybe he had been knowing right along when payrolls were due."

Tallman mused out loud. "Now, wouldn't that make a wonderful mess. The division superintendent . . . !"

Hanawalt knew who Volpondo was, Sargent thought. *No. That was no good. He also knew that Volpondo was no longer working for Western. Every picture that seemed clear at first always developed a large flaw immediately.*

"We'll check into it," Tallman said, started to leave, and then returned. "I talked to Carstairs. He was woke up by the shots the night Clum was watching the herd and you were in your room. Carstairs could hear Pete singing down by the river, but not long after the shots Brand came riding in . . . from the direction of town. Gin generally sleeps like an Indian's dog. They laugh about it, but that time he was awake. He saw Brand come in, drink some coffee . . . and clean his pistol. He put three loads back into it." Tallman let it soak all the way through before he added: "It could be he figured you another express investigator, Sargent, getting too close, right on the heels of the Volpondo killing."

For a few moments it took the ground from under Sargent. Brand was dead, and that left Sargent lunging against nothing, if Brand had killed Pat Volpondo. "Where was Brand the day Pat was shot?"

"Riding up that way . . . somewhere, Whitey says."

"Gray horse?"

"Grulla, Whitey says. So does Pete."

"I'll still be around," Sargent said.

Chapter Fourteen

Three days later Sargent was able to go down the stairs. He could not have gone sooner because Morton had just brought back his laundered clothes. They needed washing badly enough, Sargent admitted, but now the gray horse hairs that had been in his shirt were gone. He squinted hard as he went down the street toward a new sign: **Desert Cafe.**

It was mid-morning. Hadley was alone at the counter, drinking coffee, sucking absently at his stained white mustache. Sargent was hardly seated before Hadley threw a nickel on the counter and scurried out. *Pete and Ozanne are still in town,* Sargent thought. He blinked when he saw a row of Morton's stagecoaches on a shelf behind the counter. He was still looking at them when Alma Burent came from the kitchen. She did not say she was glad to see him well again, or ask how he felt. She merely looked at him.

"You don't like me much, do you?" he asked.

"We have steaks and beef stew today, Mister Sargent."

He grinned, and then glanced at the coaches. "Selling them?"

"Yes." Alma looked at the front windows.

She was expecting Ozanne and Weston any time, Sargent figured. "It won't be in here," he said.

She waited for his order. The strain lines were gone from her face now, but there was a tenseness in her manner that had sprung up the moment she came from the kitchen and saw him sitting at the counter. Not a pretty girl, not exactly that, but better looking than the picture he had been carrying of her in his mind. Monica was beautiful. This girl . . . ?

"You did come here to eat, Mister Sargent?"

"Oh, yes. A steak will do." He watched her walk back to the kitchen, and heard her talking to Mrs. Dunstan.

He swung around as the door latch clacked. Wayne Hitchcock was coming in. Two small boys were watching Sargent through the windows. Kids knew quickly when a fight was building. Hitchcock limped over to the end stool nearest the street. Fine hair was beginning to sprout around the long scar on his head. "Still around, I see, Sargent."

"Yeah." While Alma was bringing service, Sargent moved up the counter to sit beside Hitchcock. "Do you know Marty Packard, Hitchcock?"

Hitchcock's gaunt face came around slowly. "The Turret marshal? Sure. He always hangs around the trains to see who's coming in and who's leaving town . . . especially when it's someone he's told to leave Turret. Why?"

"Just wondering. Does the Smuggler have a crew of guards to take over a payroll when it hits Turret?"

"Yes. They take over from the express office, after the money is counted and signed for."

"Who signs for the Smuggler?"

"Joe Millington, the superintendent."

"Is he a friend of Packard's?"

"I wouldn't know. I don't get off the train in Turret, Sargent."

"I'm wondering if Millington knows when a payroll is coming."

"He would, I suppose." Hitchcock nodded. "He'd have to be there himself and have the guards."

"Who would tell him . . . and how?"

"That would be between Hanawalt and Millington."

"Wire? Letter?"

"I don't know," Hitchcock said. "I'm only the messenger on that run . . . or was."

From the corner of his eye, Sargent saw Alma standing just inside the kitchen doorway. He looked directly at her. Cold, white fear was on her face, and then she turned away. It puzzled Sargent, and now he knew that the first night, when she had hit him with that vengeance talk, she had not been running on incoherently because of grief alone. His mind went down a dark side trail, into thoughts with sickening implications. Hitchcock was watching him narrowly. He, too, had seen Alma's face.

"Don't give Alma trouble, Sargent." Hitchcock's voice was low, his blue eyes glassy cold. There was a feeling of strength behind his face that reminded Sargent of old Fletcher Hitchcock, handling Pete Weston.

"I don't aim to, Hitchcock."

Alma came out and drew a cup of coffee for Hitchcock. She had regained her composure, but, when Hitchcock smiled at her, she did not respond.

"I wonder," Sargent said, "if you could remember any of the names of the men who blew up the express car three years ago at Costilla Pass?"

"No! I don't want to remember their

names, or anything else about that deal."
The bitterness in Hitchcock was savage.

When Sargent watched him limp out a
few minutes later, once he'd finished his
coffee, he felt sorry for the man. Hitchcock
loved Alma Burent, and every minute he
must be thinking of that, and comparing
himself to other men who walked normally.
Wayne Hitchcock had no stagecoaches to
smash upon the floor.

The steak came. Hadley darted back and
forth before the window, and then went up
the street again. *The old man probably was
worrying more than Weston about getting the
fight started,* Sargent reflected.

He was surprised when Alma did not return to the kitchen. She leaned against the
backbar and watched him. "You're still
thrusting and pushing into something that
isn't your business, Mister Sargent."

"I think part of it is. Do you hate everybody that's trying to clear up the robbery?"

"The rest are getting paid . . . or doing
it because they must. You are just out
for . . . !"

"I know. Vengeance."

"Brand killed your friend. Why don't you
leave?"

"What makes you think he did?"

"Everybody knows it."

"I don't," Sargent said. "I'm not satisfied at all."

"Ulysses has told you about his peach trees, I know. He has worked for years to do something that would be useful. I have more admiration for him, even if he fails, than for a man who would work for years just to kill another man. You don't even want vengeance, Mister Sargent. You were going to be a rancher here, and then Brand killed your friend, and that changed your plans and made you sorry for yourself. Now, just like Pete Weston fights to make himself think he has accomplished something, you intend to kill a man to make yourself think you have served a useful purpose. You're not much of a man, Mister Sargent, just a brute carrying a gun with a deadly expression on your face."

"I'm sorry it strikes you that way, Miss Burent."

"Now . . . say . . . a man has to do what he has to do. But, if you say that to me, I'll hit you with this sugar bowl!" She turned suddenly and went back into the kitchen. Sargent heard Mrs. Dunstan say: "*Tck! Tck! Alma, girl!*"

Sargent stared at his steak. She had hit him right down the line of thought that had been growing for several days. Still, a man must do what he thought he had to do. He put a dollar on the counter and went out.

The two boys at the window began talking to him at the same time.

"Pete Weston says to hell with you. He ain't gonna bother to whip you. . . ."

"Chuck Ozanne said that," the other interrupted. "He says . . . !"

Sargent pointed inside. "See those coaches, boys? How'd you like to have one apiece?" He gave one of the boys a banknote and pointed inside again. The two boys stared at each other, and then they hit the door at the same time.

Boley Adams, dealing the poker game in The Crusher Saloon, gulped when he saw Sargent. His eyes went to the bar, and by that Sargent knew Ozanne and Weston had been here not long before. The squat, black-browed engineer, Gipp, was in the game. The same train crew that had been here the night of the robbery must be laying over again. Sargent nodded at Gipp, inclining his head toward the front.

They talked at the end of the bar. Gipp said: "Sure, the same two brakemen. Right there in the game."

Two men came over when Gipp called their names: Graefe and Bradley.

"Yeah, we seen it dumped into the

wagon," Bradley said. He looked back at the poker table, impatient.

"How far away were you?" Sargent asked.

"Maybe twenty feet," Graefe said. "It was unloaded all right, don't you worry about that."

Sargent nodded. "The same messenger that took over here that night . . . is he on the run today?"

"Number Twenty-Seven at the Lava, Jack Zellers. He's got a sour belly today," Gipp said.

Zellers was in his undershirt, holding a box of baking soda, smacking his lips distastefully. Something in Mason City, at the north end of his run, had poisoned him, he said. It was so bad he couldn't even play poker this trip, and how could a man make a living as an express messenger if he couldn't play poker now and then. The lousy company was. . . .

"The night of the robbery you saw the safe unloaded?"

"Sure, I saw it." Zellers dumped soda into a glass of water and stirred it with his finger. He belched.

"You were late, as usual?"

"I make the train. What business is it of yours?"

"How do you handle those safes?"

"On three pipes, rollers. What business have you got asking?"

"You didn't mention to Hanawalt that you were a little late . . . as usual, did you?"

Zellers started to drink, and then put down the glass. *The more a man cussed his job the less he was able to part with it,* Sargent thought. That was on Zeller's face right now.

"You work for the company?" he asked.

"No. I don't care how late you make the car. Just how much had the poker game delayed you the night of the robbery?"

"The wagon was just ready to leave, and Hitchcock was grumbling."

"You saw the safe?"

"In the wagon."

"It was *the* safe?"

"Sure! I've handled a thousand of 'em."

No good, Sargent thought, *like some other hunches that would not come off. But he was not through yet. Stubborn. Deadly, Alma had called it.*

Billy Williams, the Weston telegraph operator, was about seventy, a compact little man whose face had settled into the mask of smugness that goes with long security in a small position. One glance was enough to tell Sargent that Billy Williams did not give a hang about the public.

"Who are you?" he asked, when Sargent asked about his seeing the safe unloaded. Sargent told him.

He shook his head. "I ain't got nothing to say to nobody without authority. Now, unless you got a wire, or some other business, you're tracking sand on my floor."

Sargent leaned out from the sliding window that fronted on the track. He looked down the platform to where the express car must have stopped. It was about a hundred feet. "From here you saw it, huh?"

"I ain't saying."

"I see. You were wandering away from the office, out there . . . ?"

"I wasn't!"

"Thanks. Nice day, Mister Williams."

"I ain't. . . ." The operator grabbed a broom and began to sweep up the sand Sargent had tracked in.

That left Theobold, and he had been on the roof of the hotel, three blocks from the station. Not much use there, but Sargent went to see him anyway. Theobold was not around.

Sargent went past The Crusher Saloon, the store, and the Desert Cafe. He crossed the street and went down to Morton's livery stable.

"Sargent!" Hadley was standing at the corner of the stable near the wagon yard. He beckoned.

They would be in the yard, most likely, Sargent thought. Weston was. Ozanne was just around the corner, flattened to the wall, his pistol out.

"No need of that," Sargent said.

"Unload him, Hadley."

Hadley was already taking Sargent's gun, sucking nervously on his mustache.

"Now ain't that a pretty thing for a man to carry?" Ozanne said when Hadley took the knife. "A man? Wait till Pete gets done with him."

Ozanne has been drinking, Sargent decided, *but he is not drunk. Bringing the trouble to a head here in the wagon yard, with only Hadley as a witness . . . the thing had a murderous smell.*

Hadley was bustling importantly. "You just leave your pistol right here, too, Ozanne," he said. "We got to have things fair."

"Sure," Ozanne said, and dropped his pistol belt.

"Come on!" Weston went past the wagons to the open place near Morton's peach tree.

Sargent followed, with Hadley and Ozanne walking behind him.

Weston stopped, hunching his shoulders, rolling the knuckles of one hand in the palm of the other. "I like it better with lots of people to watch me, Chuck. I still don't see why. . . ."

"It's a little different this time, Pete," Ozanne said.

Sargent heard a meaty chop, a thump. He glanced behind him. Hadley was on the ground, his mouth open, his eyes batting in surprise. Ozanne kicked him in the temple. Hadley was still. "Take him, Pete," Ozanne said, smiling.

For a moment Weston stared at Hadley. It was obvious that Ozanne's move against Hadley had caught Weston off-balance. He was trying now to understand, but his mind was geared to a fight, and so he moved in on Sargent.

Sargent stepped back, tearing open his shirt with both hands. If he lasted at all, he would need all the air he could get, and the only way he could last very long was to hammer Weston and stay away from him.

Brock Sargent weighed one hundred and ninety pounds. His strength began in square-tipped fingers and ran clear through his body, big bones, flat muscles. He knew he was no match for the grinning, broken-nosed giant coming at him, and he had to keep one eye on Ozanne, if he could. Weston pawed with his big hands half closed. He was in no hurry. Sargent threw his left hand out to block what appeared to be a blow. Weston caught the wrist, set himself, and hauled.

Sargent could not help himself. Weston jerked him forward, let go, and Sargent went past the huge blond man and sprawled into the muddy depression around the peach tree. For a moment Sargent thought his shoulder was dislocated.

Weston stood there grinning. "You don't hold your feet so good, Sargent. You ain't going to be much fun."

Sargent slipped into the mud again when he was rising.

"Club footed," Weston said. "This ain't going to be much, Ozanne."

Not bothering to shake the mud from his hands, Sargent went into Weston, who was not even angry now. Sargent hit him in the jaw so hard that Weston's hat flew off. The next punch rocked Weston's head back and shook his mass of gold-colored curls.

Weston grinned. "That was pretty good." He began to beat down Sargent's guard. Each blow was like the crush of a greenwood club. *That wouldn't do,* Sargent thought. His arms were already aching from those two blows he had slammed into Weston's jaw, aching clear to the shoulder sockets. And he hadn't made a dent!

Ducking low, he came up under Weston's flailing arms. He pivoted a right hand in from the hips and shoulder, with all he had behind it. It took Weston just above the belt buckle. The smash did not sink. It bounced, and the pain raced up Sargent's arm again.

The next thing he knew he was lying against the peach tree, with his head ringing. At that moment he doubted that any man in the world could lick Pete Weston with his hands. All there was to do was try — and stay away from him while trying.

Sargent crawled out of the mud, and he saw that Pete was surprised to see him make it. There was hope in that. You could break a man's heart if you got up enough times when you shouldn't have risen at all. Weston decided he had wasted too much time. He rushed, swinging his right arm wide. Rough wool raked Sargent's cheek. The forearm came on through and split the side of Sargent's mouth.

He had already leaned into his punch, aiming at Weston's left eye. The blow was a trifle low. It caught Weston's cheek, and the mud and the force of the punch ripped flesh to the bone. Then Weston knew he was in a fight. He tried to close in. Sargent caught him twice in the left eye, and leaped away.

"Don't let him box!" Ozanne said. "Get hold of him!"

That was Weston's intention. He came forward with his hands open, hulking high. Once more Sargent jabbed the left eye, smearing mud and blood into it from his knuckles. It would close now, he was sure. For the first time he thought he had a chance. He moved back, circling.

"Hellsfire, Pete!" Ozanne cried. "Get him."

Weston ducked his head and rushed. Sargent got one hand against the curly head in time to keep from taking the full force of the butt. He pushed himself aside, but there was still enough power to knock him down. Weston kept going until he fell into the depression around the tree. He slipped as he was rising, and grabbed a limb. His weight split it from the tree.

Peaches thumped the mud around him as he fell. He staggered up and grabbed another limb in insane anger, and this time deliberately tore it loose. And now there were two long wounds shining against the tree trunk.

Weston's left eye was almost puffed shut. He was grizzly-angry now, but with a calculating expression of respect for Sargent in his one good eye. Sargent kept circling to the right, keeping the pressure on the closed eye, trying for the other one. Each blow he landed sent a solid shock up his arm, but he knew he would never get Weston off his feet.

"Rush him!" Ozanne said.

Sargent was in too close. Weston hauled him closer, clubbing with his right hand. The lamp almost went out on Sargent. He felt Weston's arms crushing into his back. He got one boot on Weston's toes, and let himself fall, twisting with what little leverage he had. They hit side by side.

Doubling his knees against the heavier man, Sargent drove the heels of his hands into Weston's face and tried to roll clear, but Weston grabbed his arm and hauled him back. They rolled over once, and then again, until they were lying on Hadley's legs. Hadley did not stir. Sargent broke the grip on his arm by driving his elbow into Weston's mouth.

He rolled away, and staggered up. His shirt was a muddy rag. He had time for a glance at Ozanne, just long enough to see something chilling on the dark face, to see that Ozanne was tapping his palm with a piece of leather. Then Weston came lunging in again.

Sargent was tired. His legs were going, and he knew it, but there seemed no end to Weston's strength. A grazing blow flung Sargent back until he bumped hard against a wagon hub. He hung there for a moment with his hands clutching the weathered oak of the spokes. Weston was coming in.

"Finish him!" Ozanne said.

That wagon wheel behind him . . . ! Sargent moved ahead, simulating utter exhaustion. Weston lowered his head and charged. Sargent dropped on his hands and knees. A boot took him in the side and made him gasp in agony. He heard the crack of Weston's head against the spokes, and could not move to get away from the weight that was going to come down.

Weston did not fall. He locked his arms into the spokes and hung there. By the time Sargent was on his feet, Weston was facing him, foggy-eyed, still ready to fight. They pounded each other without strength. It was a question of whether they would fall together or away from each other.

With his head against Weston's sweat-strong, heaving chest, Sargent worked his arms weakly. He heard a solid thud. It came again. Weston sagged. The thud came once more. Sargent reeled away and fell into a sitting position as Weston went down.

Ozanne was standing there with the leather in his hand; but it was not a strip of leather, after all. It was the lead-loaded end of a whip. Ozanne's lips were smiling. His eyes said murder as he walked toward Sargent.

It was all there now, from the blow and the kick that had left Hadley unconscious up to the raps that had dropped Weston when he was so groggy he would never be able to remember why he had fallen. Pete Weston would get the blame for everything.

Ozanne did not speak. He had something to do, and a witness might show up any time.

Sargent did not think he had the will to move, but he had to. He kept turning on his thighs, keeping his face toward Ozanne. Time pushing against him, Ozanne swung the whip butt. He was forced to lean down when he made his reach at Sargent's head.

Sargent drove his boot heels against Ozanne's knees. That locked the hinges and drove Ozanne back. He fell, dropping the whip butt as he snarled in pain. Sargent

scrambled away, half crawling, then stagger-
ing toward the broken peach tree limbs. He
fell just as he reached one, but he had time
to grab a limb and thrust out the bushy end
before Ozanne got to him. Ozanne slashed
down at Sargent's knees. The branch
stopped the blow, and Ozanne's sleeve
ripped as he pulled the blackjack free. He
tried to pull the limb away, but Sargent held
to it with desperate strength.

Before long Ozanne would get through
with his lead-loaded leather. Sargent knew
that, but the limb was all he had.

He was sitting in the mud, pivoting on
his buttocks, fending with the limb. Ozanne
started to circle him when the first shouts
of the crowd broke around the corner of
Morton's stable. Ozanne put the whip butt
under his shirt and walked over to Pete
Weston, lying on the ground.

Ozanne was standing there, shaking his
head, when the first two people came from
behind the wagons and got a clear view of
the scene. They were the two wide-eyed
boys, now with varnished stagecoaches under their arms. And then the crowd
swarmed in.

Ozanne grinned at the men looking down
at Weston. "First time I ever saw Pete
licked," he said.

"By Ned!" a man cried in an aggrieved tone. "We plumb missed the whole works! What happened to old Hadley?"

"He kept getting in the way," Ozanne said. "I had to rap him one."

"That done it!" someone said disgustedly. "Otherwise we'd have heard his screeching and knowed what was up. Somebody licks Pete, and we get cheated out of seein' it!"

Sargent tried to pull himself up by holding to the torn tree. He could not make it. Boley Adams and Gipp helped him rise. Boley was chewing a cigar to a pulp. "I wish I'd seen it!" he said. "I wish I had!"

Monica ran against Sargent before he saw her. She threw her arms around him. "You did it, Brock! You kicked Pete!" She pushed Boley aside and took Sargent's arm. Men were pounding his back, shouting questions. He wanted to get away as quickly as he could.

Wayne Hitchcock and Theobold and Alma came through the crowd. "Look at that tree," Alma said.

Monica laughed. "Who cares about a crazy man's pet bush?"

She and Gipp led Sargent from the yard.

At the corner of the stable Sargent said: "I'll make it now. Thanks, Gipp." He bent to pick up his knife and gun, and nearly fell.

He started into the stable. Monica tugged the other way. "Morton's out on the Middle Fork, staring into his cañon. You can't take care of yourself. Come up where I'm staying. Missus Dunstan won't mind."

"I do." Sargent disengaged her hand and walked unsteadily toward the steps.

"All right, stubborn!" She followed.

"No, Monica."

Wayne Hitchcock came by with Alma. They glanced at the scene and went on.

Theobold started to pass, then turned into the stable and took Monica's arm. "Let the man go lick his wounds," he said, smiling. Monica tried to pull away, but Theobold kept smiling, and finally he took her away.

The steps were long, steep. Upstairs, Sargent looked into the yard. Men were stepping over Hadley to look at Weston. Ozanne was grinning, talking. Hadley stirred, and someone, rather absently, helped him to his feet.

Then Weston came up in the middle of a knot of men, his tousled curls above all the other heads. He leaned against the wagon, pushing away men who tried to help him. In a few moments he walked off with Ozanne. Sargent knew that, unless someone told him, Weston would never know what had happened after he rammed the wheel.

Doc Cobb recruited two men to help Hadley. The wagon yard was soon deserted, baking in the sun. The bright scars on the peach tree stared accusingly at Sargent. He kicked the door shut, locked it, and lay down on his bed.

Later he was thankful for the two buckets of water he had carried up that morning. He was lying naked on the bed when Morton came in. The gray man said nothing until after he had dug into a trunk and found clothes for Sargent.

"One of the kids you bought coaches for said he thought for a second you and Ozanne were fighting over a limb."

"Kid talk," Sargent said. "I'm sorry about the limbs."

"Trees grow easily," Morton said.

Sargent thought: *What else does he mean that he didn't say?*

Doc Cobb came in while Sargent was dressing. He made him lie down again and examined him.

"I'm damned!" he said. "You got only cuts and bruises." He lifted Sargent's right forearm. "That's a fearful piece of bone and tissue, but I still don't see how it stopped a bull like Weston. How many times did he butt that wagon wheel?"

"Once."

"He must have raked it sidewise. He's got lumps from blows that would have killed a man with an ordinary skull, but there's only one cut on his head." Cobb pushed wet cotton that stung like a million ant bites on Sargent's torn cheek. "Whiskey. Yes, that's it. He'd been drinking. Whiskey helped you lick him, Sargent."

"I guess so." Sargent was thinking that Chuck Ozanne was a demon rider in the rocks, undoubtedly a first-class roper, and perhaps he had believed that Pat Volpondo was on his way to Weston County to investigate a conspiracy.

Dusk was coming when Sargent and Morton went to the Desert Cafe to eat. Monica was there, drinking coffee. She wrinkled her nose at Sargent. "I embarrassed you this afternoon, didn't I?"

Sargent started to grin, until his split cheek stopped him. "Forget it." She had made him feel silly before a crowd of men, but now, looking at her, it was all right.

Morton took a stool three removed from them. Alma chatted with him, telling him that Gipp and some of the other railroaders wanted coaches saved for them until the next payday. She said no more than necessary to Monica and Sargent.

Morton's eyes followed Alma as she moved back and forth between the kitchen and the counter. There was a light on his face when he was looking at Alma. It came to Sargent that several men in Weston thought highly of Alma Burent, and it built an uneasy anger in him that Morton — and others — looked down their noses at Monica Hardin.

The train was whistling in when Sargent and Monica left the cafe together. Monica said: "Let's go down to Missus Dunstan's house and talk."

Arm in arm they walked through the darkness. Before they had gone very far, Monica stopped and turned her body to him and put her arms around his neck. He sucked in his breath when she touched bruised ribs, and then he forgot the ribs.

A little later, when they were walking again, she said: "It's nice and quiet where we're going."

Chapter Fifteen

Sheriff Tallman hailed from below in the stable sometime in the middle of the night, and then he came up, clumping wearily on the steps. Morton was up and had lit a lamp before Tallman reached the room. Sargent swung stiffly out of bed.

"No reason why anybody should sleep," Tallman said. "I don't." He flopped into a chair before he noticed Sargent's face. "I see you found Pete."

"He found him," Morton said, "and he left him lying right out there in my wagon yard."

"The hell!" Tallman said. He grinned. "I wish I had been there to see that." His pleasure did not last long. "I rode the edge of the lava all day before I found out that Hanawalt went back to Turret on a light engine this afternoon. Those express boys got a regular camp out there. Still digging." Tallman shook his head. "What I started to say, Sargent, is that we wanted to see Hanawalt again and maybe the marshal of Turret." His voice was casual. "Maybe we ought

215

to go up now. I don't feel much like riding any more tonight, but we can catch the westbound in a half hour. What do you think?"

Sargent looked at his right hand. It was swollen, cut. He could hardly bend the fingers. If he and Tallman walked in on Marty Packard together, it might tip things into a showdown — too soon. Whatever Packard was, Sargent was sure he was tough. Sargent could not let Tallman carry the fight alone, and that was the way it would be if they went up there now.

"Let's wait," Sargent said. "I don't feel like making the trip right now."

Tallman nodded. He seemed relieved. "I stopped by the station on the way here. Two messages. Volpondo's sorrel stallion showed up several days ago at Trinchera. No saddle. No bridle. Rock scars healing on his legs. Bad rope burn on the neck." There was silence. Tallman rubbed his hand across his eyes, yawning. "The other message was from a lawyer in Alder," he continued. "Volpondo left a will . . . everything he had goes to you, I gathered. The lawyer wanted to know if I had found any money on him."

Sargent remembered the day they had gone to the lawyer's office six years before, each having a will drawn in favor of the other. Afterward, they had laughed about it.

Tallman rose. "Don't come around to see me before afternoon." He went slowly down the steps.

Sargent looked at Morton. "Do you remember the names of the three men Volpondo and Tallman cleaned up in the Sodas?"

Morton blew out the lamp. His voice came gloomily from the darkness. "No, I don't remember. Why didn't you ask Tallman?" A moment later he asked: "Volpondo was in on that, huh?"

Sargent had curried Windy and was at the water trough the next morning when Fletcher Hitchcock and Whitey Fallon came across the street, the foreman moving awkwardly beside the long-striding Triangle owner.

Hitchcock put one foot on the trough, looking at Windy's shining coat and clean, powerful lines. He gave a small, involuntary nod of appreciation, and then he pushed his hat back and looked at Sargent.

Fallon was standing a few paces to one side of his employer, his blistered face without expression. *They make a pair,* Sargent thought. *If Hitchcock said suddenly: 'Shoot this man, Whitey,' the foreman would blink, and then start carrying out the order.*

"You satisfied about that fight, Sargent?" Hitchcock asked.

"Sure. I was lucky. I'm satisfied. Why?"

"There's been talk. One of the kids took a shortcut under a wagon, and he's been saying something about Ozanne trying to hit you with a limb."

"He shoved it at me to help me up," Sargent said.

Hitchcock and Fallon looked at each other. In silence they agreed not to swallow that one.

"Pete's fair, even if he is a hellion at times," Hitchcock said. "I like to keep everything about Triangle that way. I want you to know, if Ozanne jumped you after you'd got Pete stopped . . . I wouldn't like that, Sargent."

Sargent watched Fallon. "Why should he jump me?"

"Monica," Hitchcock said.

Ever since the fight Sargent had wondered if jealousy would be enough to make a man try murder. He had decided that in Ozanne's case, it was enough. And still, he thought there might be other reasons.

"Pete was never one to sneak his troubles away where no one could see it," Hitchcock resumed. "Hadley suddenly gets knocked out. It all smells bad to me, Sargent. I want to know the truth. Did the two of them try to kill you?"

Hitchcock's voice betrayed him. He was desperate to know. Sargent realized it was not Ozanne he was worrying about. He could fire Ozanne with a word. But it was grinding hard in Hitchcock to know whether or not Pete Weston, the replacement of an only son, had been involved in murder and robbery. Sargent wanted to say that Weston was completely in the clear about the robbery; but he did not know.

Fallon wet his lips. "One little thing, Sargent . . . Pete didn't bust Morton here that day. He shoved him out of the way. Ozanne hit him."

Hitchcock waited for his answer.

Sargent said: "Whitey, I know you must have tried to backtrack Pete to see where he went the day Volpondo was killed. Hitchcock told you to do it. What did you find out?"

Fallon looked at his boss. Hitchcock nodded.

"He might have got over in the East Fork country that day," Fallon replied. "Dry ground. The age of tracks are hard to judge. I don't think he did, from what I could tell."

"But you're not sure?" Sargent asked.

"That's right," Hitchcock said. "Pete is the only son I ever had." It was bleak, final, cutting Wayne Hitchcock from existence. "But if he killed a man, or was in on that robbery, he might as well be a stranger . . . as far as I'm concerned."

Little items added up in Sargent's mind to say that Weston knew nothing about the robbery, but they were only guesses strung together. It was the look on Hitchcock's face that made him say: "I don't see Pete in this thing at all." He hoped he was right.

Tenseness melted on Hitchcock's gaunt face. Tight lines around the eyes loosened. "Sargent, the way I stack it up, you seem to be the only man that outlaw bunch is afraid of. I'm glad to hear what you just said. Come on, Whitey."

Hitchcock strode away.

"Just a minute, Whitey," Sargent said. "What else did you find in the East Fork country?"

Fallon looked at Hitchcock's receding back. The old man was striding away with a straight, proud set in his shoulders.

"Ah . . . nothing much," Fallon said.

"You saw where a man held his horse behind a brush screen between big rocks, where he afterward roped a horse below the trail, and forced him back?"

"Yeah." Fallon rubbed his lips together.

"You know more about horse tracks than I do."

"You and Morton sort of messed up the sign. A man couldn't be sure of anything."

"Sure you don't know whose horse it was?"

"No . . . no, I don't know."

"Who carried a carbine that day . . . the day Bledsoe was killed? A Thirty-Thirty?"

"Boots get hung up on the rocks pretty bad," Fallon said. "In the brush, too. 'Less we want a deer, we don't generally carry short guns at Triangle."

Sargent jumped on the evasion. "Who carried one that day?"

Fallon looked again after Hitchcock's back. "Pete, damn you!" He walked away.

Sargent cursed under his breath. Nothing would come out all black or all white. He swung up bareback to give Windy exercise.

Sargent saw the sun glinting on Monica's golden hair as she walked rapidly beside a warped fence to intercept him in the main street. She patted Windy's neck when Sargent stopped. Sargent felt vaguely that there should be something different in her face,

221

a change of some kind, but she was just the same — beautiful, smiling, the same direct look in her eyes. She was wearing blue, handmade trousers.

"Get me a horse from Morton," she said. "We'll go riding. Windy acts like he needs a run."

Sargent hesitated. "Not today. I have to. . . ."

"Come on! We'll go get another horse. Let me ride Windy down to the stable."

"Not with just a halter."

"Please." She reached for the halter. "I don't often say please, Brock."

"Some other time. I have to. . . ."

"You just don't want to go riding."

"I do. That's the trouble," Sargent admitted. He got down to lead Windy. Monica grabbed the gelding's mane and started to leap up. Windy snorted and tried to rear. She held her grip and would have gone aboard anyway, if Sargent had not grabbed her around the waist.

"I'd soon break him of that!" she promised. Something hot and willful flamed in her eyes.

"No woman's ever ridden him," Sargent said.

She looked at Sargent sidewise. "I bet I can. Just watch me!"

"Some other time. Going to breakfast?"

They started walking down the middle of the street.

"Yes, I'm going down to Alma's place." She laughed, and Sargent did not understand why. "What do you think of Alma, Brock?"

"I'd say she was a nice girl."

"A *nice* girl, Brock?" Monica laughed again. "She'd never invite you down to Missus Dunstan's, would she?"

"What's the matter with you, Monica?"

"Nothing, nothing! What's the matter with you?"

Sargent studied her face. If there was any of the devilish perverseness that had flashed to the surface still in her mind at the moment, he could not tell, but he was still a little disturbed by the quick change.

"Have some coffee with me?" she suggested. "I know you probably ate breakfast before daylight. Have you always been a cowboy, Brock?"

"Mostly. Have you always been a hellion?"

"Always!"

She grabbed his hand. They laughed together, and then, swinging hands like two children, they changed course toward the livery stable. A group of railroaders just entering the Desert Cafe turned their heads to look. Morton was working in a stall. He took his pitchfork and went out the back doors of the stable, as if he had important business in the yard.

Sargent tied the halter rope to slick wood. "Have you got any ideas about the robbery, Monica?"

"Yes. There's a hundred thousand dollars lying around some place. That's a wonderful idea."

"You mean the reward for finding it?"

"If you want to play penny ante, Brock . . . ?"

"You're not serious?"

She saw the deep set of graveness change his face. "Of course not! Let's get the coffee, sober-sides."

Railroaders at the counter looked over their shoulders as Monica's trousers went by. There was one empty stool, at the end, beside Wayne Hitchcock. Monica took it. She touched Hitchcock's shoulder. "Hi there, Wayne!"

Sargent saw the shoulder jerk. "Hello, Monica," Hitchcock said in a dead voice. He went out a few moments later, leaving food on the plate.

Alma stood before them, waiting. The devil came up in Monica's face. She murmured: "Brock says you're a nice girl, Alma."

Alma blushed.

Anger, Sargent thought. *She's boiling inside.*

"Mister Sargent says lots of things, Monica."

"Not about one thing, I hope," Monica said sweetly, and smiled.

From the kitchen doorway a wispy little woman, her face red from the stove, watched Sargent and Monica for a moment with a troubled, speculative look. *Mrs. Dunstan,* Sargent knew. It was the first time he had seen her at close range. Something in her expression made him uneasy, gave him a feeling of guilt.

One of the railroaders answered a question. "Sure! If you ask me, the gold's in Old Mexico now, and someone is having a high time . . . and I only wish it was me!"

Chapter Sixteen

In mid-afternoon Sargent started toward the courthouse to see Sheriff Tallman. There were more people on the streets than he had seen in Weston before. They nodded or spoke, and some of the men would have stopped to talk about his fight with Weston, but the cast of his face made them hesitate.

The Crusher had its steady game. *Railroaders, mainly, kept the town alive,* Sargent thought. It was also the supply point for prospectors in the Sodas and for ranchers north of the Sodas. There were a few like Doc Cobb. Fifteen or twenty families of men who worked in Turret were here because there was no housing for them in the mining camp.

Develop some steady, long-lasting project here — such as Morton's orchards — and the town would be secure, Sargent now believed, never booming, but never dying either. His line of thought surprised him for he had told himself all along that he had no permanent interest in Weston. Still, it did not seem right that a hell-roaring camp

226

like Turret might someday take the court-house, with a man like Marty Packard, say, in the sheriff's job.

He was passing the Lava House when he remembered he wanted to see Theobold. The windows had been washed. Theobold, incongruous in a storekeeper's apron, was mopping the lobby. Water on the windows and on Theobold's mop had revealed tiles that had been obscured under grime and murk. Theobold put the mop in the wringer and stepped on the lever, cocking a cigar-broken grin at Sargent.

"Morton says I stir every five, six years," he said. "This must be the year. I said you insulted me, Sargent, and made me feel lazy and worthless. Care to move in again? I'll put you up on the third floor, where they'll have to use a ladder to shoot in your window."

Sargent grinned. It struck him that for ten years he had never considered himself per-manent anywhere, never had made friends. Old Gloomy Gus, pinching his nickels, hoarding his emotions. He pushed those thoughts aside. There was still grim business before he would be free to look at his future.

"You saw the safe unloaded, Theobold?"

Theobold nodded. "At quite a distance, of course."

"You never doubted that it was unloaded?"

Something changed in Theobold's face. "No," he said slowly. "No, we . . . I was really too far away to make any judgment."

"You started to say 'we.' Was there someone with you?"

Theobold raised his brows. His face was suave. "The editorial 'we,' Sargent. I didn't realize I used it. What's behind your question?"

"Nothing much." *There had been somebody with him. Why was he denying it now?*

Theobold blew smoke toward the high ceiling. "Look at that mess up there. How could a place get like that in just five or six years? I had the ceiling cleaned before, I'm sure." He grinned again. "Thought any more about the peach orchards, Sargent?"

"Not much." *Here, possibly, was the shrewdest man in Weston. Don't jump at conclusions,* Sargent thought. "Thanks for the information, Theobold. No 'we'?"

"Just me." Theobold began mopping the floor again.

Two men were tearing down the rotting fire escape at the side of the hotel. In the street was a pile of new fir timber. Four or five spectators were watching the carpenters, giving advice.

Sheriff Tallman and Hadley were doing something near the ditch in front of the courthouse. When Sargent got closer, he saw they had run water to the dying locust trees and were flooding the baked lawn.

"Why did Ozanne hit me?" Hadley asked. "I missed the best fight there's ever been around here. I helped them arrange it so's a crowd wouldn't bother them, and then. . . ."

"He figured you'd talk 'em both to death before they had a chance to scrap," Tallman said. He dropped his shovel. "You keep the water going, Hadley. Me and Sargent. . . ."

Hadley protested: "You don't run the whole courthouse, Tallman."

"I won't let you listen at my door any more, Hadley, if you don't. . . ."

"So! You accuse me of listening at doors!" Hadley dropped his shovel in the ditch. "To hell with you, Tallman." He walked away.

Tallman spat. "How'd you like to be county clerk, Sargent? You can also be sheriff, if you want to, the way they're bellowing up in Turret about me. Last year they had me licked, the year before, too, but they got to scrapping among themselves and put up four candidates. . . . Not interested in politics, huh? Well, let's get on with the robber chasing."

They sat down in the shade on the court-house steps.

"Energy's catching," Tallman resumed. "Theobold starts to fix his steps, and I start watering the trees. Pretty soon they'll paint the railroad station, and then the boom will be over for another five years. What's on your mind this morning?"

"Marty Packard."

Tallman nodded. "I been thinking . . . can we bring him in, on the word of a dead man?"

Sargent had been wondering about other obstacles in the way of bringing Packard in.

"By the way," Tallman added, "I sent Morton out the other day and had him bury Bledsoe. Somebody beefs 'em, we plant 'em. That seems to be the extent of things."

Sargent laughed.

Tallman said: "You're getting damned near human. What's happened to you?" And then something ran in his eyes, and he looked away, and both of them knew his thoughts.

Sargent said: "I guess you're right. Taking Packard out of his own nest might be a job."

"I've tackled worse. But we can't hold him long, and he'll know it. So what can we get out of him?"

Water gurgled faintly in the yard. The carpenters across the street pulled loose a timber with a screeching of rusty nails.

Tallman continued: "What this kid has been saying about Ozanne the day you and Weston fought. . . ."

"He was right." Sargent told the whole story.

"Hmm." Tallman frowned. "Just where does that put Ozanne? One reason for wanting to get rid of you . . . or a nice big double reason?"

"I'm not sure."

"Haven't you found out yet?"

Sargent got it soon enough. Tallman thought he was playing Monica for information about Ozanne. Sargent felt heat rising in his neck.

"Excuse that one," Tallman said quickly. "A man can make a mistake." And then, quite carefully, he said: "I got it indirectly that Fletch Hitchcock kicked Monica off the Triangle. Indirectly, hell! Missus Sommers was in town a few days ago. She told me. Fletch said he would support Monica until she got married, but he didn't want her around Triangle any longer. Everything Fletch has goes to Pete Weston, with Fallon holding the strings. Monica and Wayne get five bucks apiece. She told you, I suppose."

Sargent nodded. He wondered why Monica had not told him. He asked: "Was there anyone on the roof with Theobold the night the safe came in?"

Tallman grunted. "Not that I know about. Why?"

"He slipped a little when I was talking to him, and I thought he might have covered something up."

"Why would he? He was three blocks away. What could he have seen that the others didn't?" Tallman was silent for some time. "What you seem to be poking into would sort of fit with what I've been saying . . . that the safe ain't in the desert . . . or on the lava . . . or anywhere out there." Tallman rose suddenly. "Let's you and me take a ride out into the lava. I want to show you a few things, get your opinion . . . and I think Hanawalt may be around the express company camp."

On their way to the stable Sargent saw Monica at the Lava House desk, talking to Theobold. When he and Tallman passed the Desert Cafe, Mrs. Dunstan came out and called to Sargent. Tallman went on toward the stable.

Mrs. Dunstan was twisting her hands in her apron. She was flustered, but still she was determined to say what was on her mind. "Mister Sargent, I don't approve of men visiting alone with someone who is staying at my house. I have told Monica that, and she moved. You understand . . . well, people say I'm an excitable woman and things like that, but I know what I'm doing. I've been ill, Mister Sargent. The night of the robbery here I thought I was dying, and I sent for the minister, Mister Theobold. I've done silly things like that, perhaps, but I know my mind. I won't have men visiting. . . ."

"I understand, Missus Dunstan," Sargent said gravely.

"I hope you won't think I'm an excitable woman. My husband always said. . . ."

Sargent got away after a while. He was almost to the stable doors before something caught in his mind. Alma Burent had gone to get Theobold the night of the robbery. He had been on his roof. They had been there together when the train came in. Why was there anything in that to hide?

Tallman had heard Mrs. Dunstan's chattering, but he said nothing until he and Sargent were riding toward the Sodas.

"Alma, huh? . . . on the roof with Tracy that night?"

They followed a broad trail through the sand, marked by little potholes and the evidence of camp sites. Midway to the Sweet-water they came to the first camp, a wagon sheet spread on four wobbly poles above equipment. A man was sleeping on his back, his snores disturbing flies around his bearded mouth.

Four others were scattered along the trail toward the Sodas, probing at the sand with bars. Tallman looked at the sleeping man. He sighed, and drew his pistol. The shot brought the man from slumber in a rush. He knocked down one of the poles and wallowed under enveloping canvas before he got clear.

"Any developments, Earl?" Tallman asked.

The man looked sheepish. He brushed sand off his sweat-soaked undershirt. "Naw, nothing."

"That's a good deputy," Tallman said gently. "Go back to sleep, Earl. They'll be sure to tell you if they find the gold."

Sargent was still laughing silently when they were a hundred yards from the camp.

"That's a nice hammer you got there, Jim," Tallman said to a man they passed. "Figure on cracking walnuts?"

"I got hopes." The man grinned. "Why don't you take a little vacation, Morse? A man would figure you think some of us boys dishonest."

They passed several more camps, more men. Some of them, Tallman said, were miners who had quit their jobs in Turret, figuring that their talents underground had fitted them for discovering gold in a highly concentrated form out here in the desert.

A half mile from the river, Tallman stopped. He pointed back toward Weston. "Up to here, the four horses came along right brisk, never a pause. There wasn't a sign that a man had got down to tighten a cinch . . . or nothing. They stayed pretty much in a square formation."

"Pretty much? They'd have to stay together tight and square with that load."

"Yeah, I know. They didn't vary much, but that little is what's been troubling me." Tallman put his palms a few inches apart, then sawed his hands back and forth. "Seven hundred pounds in the middle of a rack couldn't stand too much of that."

Near the river they rode into a wash that grew wider and steeper as it approached the water. Tallman reined in and pointed at a high bank. "They dropped it right there." The bank had been scarred and probed and tunneled. "The sign showed the horses got in a mess. The safe fell off the rack. One man got down, put a rope on it, and they dragged it up to that bush with a horse. . . ." Tallman blinked. "Well, there was a bush there once."

"Only one man got down?" Sargent asked.

"That's the way the sign read. One man, about a number eight boot. They loaded the safe again from where the bush was and give up trying to make the bank. They went on down to the river, and then turned east to the ford."

Sargent kept studying the bank. "You saw the impression of the safe?"

"Even measured it with a piece of rope. It checked out just right."

"One man on the ground, three still on their horses. . . ." Sargent shook his head. "I'd like to see that done."

"It puzzles me, too," Tallman admitted.

They went on to the river, and turned east toward the ford a half mile upstream. All the way the river had a rock bottom, and every inch of it had been probed, Tallman said. They crossed the ford and came out on brown lava. For an hour they rode steadily across the drummy ground. Tallman stopped again in a depression, shielded by weird rocks that were eroded in the shape of squat, long-necked animals.

"Here's where the rack was burned," Tallman said. "And from here they split four ways. I picked the trail that went toward the Sodas for a while. Then it veered around and headed straight back toward town, and then the wind came up . . . and there wasn't any trail left after the sand blew a little."

Sargent got down and scraped with his boot where there was just a trace of ashes showing. He got on his hands and knees and raked with his fingers.

"Looking for nails?" Tallman asked.

Sargent gave the sheriff a quick look. "Yeah."

"I thought of that. Figured maybe they hid the safe right in Weston and decoyed out this way with a box. But the ashes weren't scattered hardly at all when I first saw this place . . . and there weren't any nails."

"They could have been pulled before the boards were burned."

"I sort of threw a study in that direction myself," Tallman said. "First time I meet somebody wearing a claw hammer in his holster. . . . This thing is making me nuts."

They rode on a short distance and struck the railroad, and then turned north along it until they came to a camp of two large tents located near the tracks. A square-set man had heard them coming and was waiting. It was McClellan, the special agent Sargent had met by accident in the Turret alley.

He grinned at Sargent. "I don't feel so bad. I hear you whipped the biggest bully boy in this end of the country, Sargent."

"You guys know everything," Tallman said. "Where's the gold?"

McClellan jerked his thumb toward the river. "Hanawalt is hot on the trail right now. What makes you think it ain't out here, Sheriff?"

"I'm the seventh son of a saddle maker," Tallman said. "I got it off the end of a leather punch at midnight. Come on, Sargent, let's find Hanawalt."

They found Mike Hanawalt, dog-trotting from one group of diggers to another. He was wearing a fine sunburn and a determined look.

"Come back to the river and bathe your feet," Tallman said.

Sargent and Tallman loosened their clothes and sat down near the water. Hanawalt paced restlessly. "One of my boys picked up a rumor last night that two miners found the safe and buried it again right close to here."

"Great country for rumor," Tallman said. "What's new in Turret?"

Hanawalt's head jerked around. "Turret is yielding nothing. I pulled my boys out of there after Bledsoe got his."

"All of them?" Sargent asked casually.

"What's on your mind?" Hanawalt asked.

"You trust Wayne Hitchcock . . . all the way," Sargent said. "He didn't signal anyone that the safe was on the train. How about the guard?"

"He read a magazine all the way from Alder to Turret," Hanawalt said. "He's my nephew. Worthless. If somebody said boo, he'd hand over his shotgun and help open the safe. Everyone knows that. That's why I sent him on that trip. With him as guard 'most anybody would figure there wasn't over two dollars' worth of anything in the express car. But it didn't work."

"You trust him as honest, though?" Sargent asked.

"He's honest. I'll give him that."

"Did Joe Millington, the Smuggler super, know the payroll was coming?" Sargent watched Hanawalt closely.

After a while Hanawalt nodded. "He knew."

"He might have dropped it, huh?" Tallman asked.

"That would have been foolish," Hanawalt said.

"He let it out, didn't he?" Tallman asked. Hanawalt nodded.

"Did he also drop something about Pat Volpondo?" Sargent asked.

Hanawalt's quick eyes studied them for several moments. He sat down suddenly. "Millington gets careless after a few drinks. Before I knew that, I sent Volpondo to check on something with him several years ago . . . about a heavy bullion shipment, it was. Later, after I learned Millington sometimes talked too much, I was sorry I'd sent Pat. I hoped Millington would forget all about him, but he didn't." Hanawalt tossed a rock toward the water. "A few months ago Millington asked me about Volpondo. Once you'd seen Pat and talked to him, you didn't forget him easy." Hanawalt nodded. "Yeah, Millington admitted to me the other day that he slipped and talked about the payroll. He didn't remember saying anything about Volpondo, but he admitted he might have."

"To Marty Packard," Sargent said.

"How'd you know?"

"Guessed it." Tallman's voice was bland. "Packard never lets anyone come back to town . . . his town, like he always says . . . after he's told 'em to light out. Bledsoe came back, and Packard knew it."

"Packard would have killed him, too," Hanawalt said. "Except that Bledsoe begged off and got on his belly."

"Oh? I see you haven't told us everything right along, Hanawalt," Tallman said.

"I thought I could handle the Packard end. I've got men watching him now, trying to establish a connection between him and the robbery."

"They didn't happen to see him ride out of town the day Bledsoe was killed, did they?" Sargent asked.

"He hasn't been out of Turret at all."

"Has anyone from down here been up to talk to him?" Sargent asked.

"Not that I know of," Hanawalt said. "I don't have a hundred special agents, you know. One of them got drunk for a day and night up there in Turret, and I lost about thirty hours' check on Packard before I found out and fired the agent." He looked defensively at Tallman. "You got a deputy out here that sleeps all the time, Sheriff."

"I'll speak to that deputy . . . by hand," Tallman said. "Go on, Hanawalt."

"That's all."

They sat by the river, not looking at each other, until Hanawalt said: "I guess you'd better bring Packard down here to jail, Tallman."

"Well," the sheriff said in a long drawl, "that's a big order. Sort of startles me. You being a U. S. deputy marshal, couldn't you get a government warrant of some kind?"

"I looked into it. The federal judge says not enough evidence . . . yet." Hanawalt stared at Tallman hard.

"You could bring him in on suspicion, Sheriff, without a warrant. He's mighty like the way your judge sounds."

"Who is your judge?" Hanawalt asked.

"Tracy Theobold."

"The hotelman?"

"Minister, hotelman, lawyer . . . almost an orchard grower. I don't think he'd issue the warrant, Hanawalt." Tallman rose. "Let's leave Packard stew for a while, huh?"

"I've changed my mind about watching him any longer," Hanawalt said. "He ought to be in jail. Otherwise, he may be lost to us . . . like Bledsoe."

Sargent was watching Hanawalt narrowly. There were times when he wanted badly to believe Hanawalt. The man was so quick, changeable. It was hard to be sure about him.

"Whoever went after Packard might be lost . . . like Bledsoe," Tallman mused.

"You could deputize Sargent, Sheriff." Hanawalt stared earnestly. "You'd go, wouldn't you, Sargent? Packard undoubtedly knows who killed Volpondo."

Sargent followed Tallman's lead. "I don't know." For a long time he had been regretting telling Hanawalt about Benny Paez. "Why don't we all three go?"

Hanawalt shook his head. "I learned my lesson the last time. I'm just no good in an open scrap."

Sargent thought: *If that was an admission, it was a very honest one.* He remembered something that had been slipping in and out of his mind for a long time. "What were the names of the gang Volpondo and Tallman took in the Sodas three years ago?"

Hanawalt said six names without hesitation. "The last three are the ones Pat and Tallman got. Prowers is doing twenty years. What's that got to do . . . ?"

"Any local men, Tallman?"

"Bart Grove worked about six months at Triangle," the sheriff said. "I never made anything of that, and old Fletch was pretty touchy about even mentioning the subject."

"Any dog can get in a kennel," Hanawalt said. "That Fletcher Hitchcock, I hear, is touchy about a lot of things." He grinned suddenly. "By the way, I hear he has a niece that. . . ."

"We'll be going now," Tallman said. "See

you in a day or two, Hanawalt."

Once more they rode past the groups of men digging in the sand, jabbing at it with bars. This area was half a mile from any part of the trail the four horses had made, Tallman said. Earl, the deputy, was sound asleep again when they passed the wagon sheet on four posts. Tallman shook his head.

"I had two deputies here," he said. "But one was honest. He got a big hammer and went looking for the safe. He did mention, when I caught up with him, that he figured to resign as soon as I came along. You want Earl's job, Sargent? Two bucks a day. All you got to do is sleep during the hot time, and play Mexican monte when it cools off. You get your money when the mines and railroad pay their taxes."

"You can deputize me just before we get to Turret."

"We'll rest the horses. We'll strike out to make Turret sometime tomorrow morning. I don't want folks to say we caught Packard in bed at Grace's dump and took unfair advantage of him. You think we got Hanawalt fooled any?"

"Maybe. They've got no horses out here, and, if another light engine doesn't come along, I don't see how Hanawalt can beat us to Turret to warn Packard . . . if he does suspect we're going up there."

"Yeah." Tallman spat. "I was about to mark Hanawalt off our list, and then he suddenly wants someone to get shot, tackling Marty Packard . . . or the other way around. That safe, sure as little green apples, is lying somewhere still full of a hundred thousand bucks, and every roached skunk that was in on the robbery is trying the gun route to make his split bigger."

The weak point in the whole structure kept sticking in Sargent's mind: *Why had the men burdened themselves with a tremendous weight of iron, when they could have broken the box close to Weston, taking only gold coin? How many men? Hitchcock said four. The horses indicated four, but only one got down when the box was dropped, and then the horses went four ways after reaching the lava. Four men?*

Two good riders, perhaps only one, using the ropes on four horses, might have gone toward the lava — with a certain kind of box. After the tracks split where the rack was burned, blowing sand obscured the trails before Tallman had been able to make a thorough check. Say there were two, or even three, riderless mounts. They sure wouldn't have stayed long on the lava after being started off in different directions.

The right kind of horses, picked for the purpose, would have gone home before daylight. Where was home?

"Why'd you want those names?" Tallman asked.

"Volpondo was probably unconscious but alive when he was tied to that stirrup. I can't see any man doing that unless he had a terrible grudge. I thought maybe one of the men you and Pat took in the Sodas. . . ."

"Yeah, Bart Grove was mighty thick with Chuck Ozanne when Grove worked at Triangle. They had been kids together down in Texas. I'll say that much, Sargent. No more. Give every man his chance, until you know."

"That leans pretty strong to me, considering other things."

"I was afraid it would," Tallman said.

Chapter Seventeen

Stripped to the waist, his muscles running in great ridges, Pete Weston was digging with a pick in Morton's wagon yard. Sweat showered out of his curly hair when he shook his head. His blocky features broke into a huge grin when he saw Sargent.

Weston came out of the hole and bumped across the yard like a bear — with his hand out. Sargent blinked at the grip, afterward looked at his hand, and grinned at Weston.

"Don't try to fool me," Weston said. "You got dynamite in that thing! I ought to know."

"What are you digging, Pete?"

Weston looked sheepish. "That's a tree hole. Fletch said to do it for bustin' Morton's tree up. I don't mind doing it, since Fletch said to, but if anybody comes around here making fun. . . ."

"They won't. I'll see to that."

Weston poked a fist against Sargent's shoulder, and Sargent tried to roll with it, but in spite of that he was forced to step back. "You ought to come out to Triangle and go to work, Sargent. It's a good place now that Monica's gone. Ozanne quit yesterday, and. . . ."

"Ozanne quit? Where'd he go?"

"I don't know."

"I'm going to tell you something, Pete, but first I want to ask you a question or two without you getting mad."

"Go ahead. Hell, if I get too mad, we can always fight again, and then I'll be all right."

Sargent laughed. "I won't be all right if we scrap again!" He watched Weston's grin and decided to go ahead. "You remember the day Bledsoe was killed? He had been hiding out . . . ?"

"Yeah. I remember."

"You carried a carbine that day, Pete, didn't you?"

Weston scowled. "Uhn-huh, I did. I was maybe going to pick me off a bear on the Middle Fork, but Chuck borrowed the carbine before we separated. He give it back that night."

"Dirty?"

"Yeah. He said he blasted a coyote."

"Did Fallon know Ozanne had borrowed it?"

"Uhn-uh. There wasn't anything to know. Chuck slipped it back into my saddle boot at the corral that night."

Ozanne. . . . Ozanne. . . . The name ran in Sargent's head and brought the fumes of rage smoking up inside, and then Sargent got himself under control. He was cold and purposeful — and close to the end of a trail.

"What was it you were going to tell me, Sargent?"

"I never licked you. I never could. You hit that wagon wheel with your head, but you weren't out. Ozanne beat you on the head three times, at least, with the butt of a teamster's whip, and then he tried to kill me."

"Chuck hit me! What for?"

"Didn't you think it funny, Pete, that he got Hadley to decoy me in here where no one could see the fight?"

"Yeah. He said he didn't want Tallman breaking it up."

"Tallman was out of town, and Ozanne knew it. He used you, Pete, just as he used you when he borrowed your carbine to kill a man."

It soaked in slowly, but, when it did, Weston was all burly rage in an instant. "I'll break him in pieces!"

"No, Pete, I want him . . . if I can find him. Tell Fletcher Hitchcock and Fallon what I've said, but no one else. Understand?"

"All right."

"Fine! Now, do you need help digging that hole?"

Weston grinned. "You're all right, Sargent. I figured to hire someone to dig it, but old Fletch, he was onto that before I thought of it. He said I'd have to dig the hole myself, so I guess I will!"

Fletcher Hitchcock might have picked a smarter son, Sargent thought, but he could have done much worse. He punched Weston in the shoulder, and Weston did not move. He only grinned.

"Let's you and me fight again sometime, Sargent, just for fun, huh?"

"If I can run, we won't fight again, Pete."

Chapter Eighteen

They would ride for Turret about midnight, Tallman had said, right after he had deputized Sargent, and that would get them into Turret about breakfast time. With good luck they would have Packard in tow and be on their way back before the mining camp knew what had happened. They would get the extra horse from a livery stable in Turret.

Those were large details. The small ones . . . Tallman had shrugged. "We'll work them out on the spot . . . I hope."

"Warrant?"

The sheriff had shaken his head. "Never used one in my life. Couldn't get it anyway, not from Theobold, with just the word of a dead robber to use."

Midnight was a long time away. Sargent left Pete Weston, sweating at his work, and went to the Desert Cafe. Only Alma and Mrs. Dunstan were there.

Sargent took no chances that Alma would rip into him again before he finished. He ate first before he said: "What did you and

Theobold see from the roof of the Lava House the night of the robbery?"

She was picking up dishes. She put them down again, and her hands trembled as she gripped the counter. Her face was sick and white. "Nothing," she said. "Nothing! Why don't you get out of here?"

"I will." Sargent thought he had better get to Theobold before she did.

The lobby of the Lava House had a different look. The metal ceiling and the oak paneling on the walls were shining clean. Theobold was at the desk, smoking a cigar. He saw the urgency in Sargent and seemed to brace himself.

"Alma just told me that you and she were on the roof the night of the robbery, Theobold."

"She did?" Theobold removed his cigar and wiped his lips with a handkerchief.

"What did you see, Theobold?"

"The train. I've watched it come in a hundred times from my roof."

"I respect Alma Burent as much as you do," Sargent said. "She's been afraid of me since the first night I came here. Why?"

"She told me you had a rather deadly look that gave her the creeps."

"Not enough, Theobold."

Theobold shrugged.

"Is she in love with Wayne Hitchcock?"

"Don't ask a third party."

"You would know."

Theobold put the cigar between his lips again. He shook his head. "She isn't, not that it's our business."

Sargent took a deep breath. "What the two of you are trying to hide is killing her inside. No honest woman or man can live with a thing like that. Let's lay it in the open, Theobold, and see what we can do about it."

Theobold stared at the counter. Then he raised his head slowly. "If I can give you something to help clear up the robbery, will you promise to come in with Morton and me on the dam and irrigation project?"

"No. Not on the basis you mention."

"I'm glad you said that, Sargent. You're stone blind in some things, but you're honest in the principles. We saw the train come in. Alma had come to get me because Missus Dunstan thought she was dying. I was rising. We both were looking toward the train. From where we were, we could see clearly into the express car. I want you to know, Sargent, that Alma and I never spoke of this together. If I concealed something, which I have, I did it because Alma Burent is one of the finest girls God ever created.

Burent and Hitchcock dumped the safe into the wagon. Before that, they lifted it from one side of the car to the other." Theobold walked around the desk. "And now I'm going up to tell Alma what I've said."

They lifted it from one side . . . to the other. Sargent watched Theobold go out. He stood at the desk for a long time, rubbing his fingers on the polished walnut. He was standing there when Monica came down the stairs and called his name with a happy cry.

He was thinking of many things but not directly of Monica, as she led him to the second floor. Once in her suite, he had to think of Monica Hardin. She put her arms around his neck and kissed him.

"What in the world were you and Theobold talking about that's made you so grim?"

"You heard some of it?"

"Well, I heard you talking, that's all. I stopped on the stairs so I wouldn't butt into a serious conversation. What's the matter, Brock?"

She was warm and pliant against him, and Sargent could not think too well. He told himself it was no time to try to think.

Later, together in bed, she stroked her fingers idly across his scarred cheek. "Chuck

Ozanne quit suddenly at Triangle. Why?"

"I don't know," Sargent said.

"You do too, I'll bet."

"Why should I know?"

Her eyes were narrow. There was a tiny run of tenseness in her voice. "Do you think he's one of the robbers?"

"What makes you ask?"

"Well, there's talk around. You know how it is."

"How is it?" he asked. "How is it in a thing like that?"

She sat up. "You're stubborn, Brock."

"I just want to know why you think Ozanne was in on the safe robbery. I haven't heard any talk."

She smiled, and her eyes were still tight. "Now I know it. Before, it was just a guess."

He grabbed her by the shoulders. "You guessed, huh?"

She did not wince. The little smile held, but her eyes were blazing. "Jealous, aren't you, Brock?"

He shook her, and then he raised his right hand to slap her. "Go ahead," she said. "I suspected there was a mean streak in you. Chuck was never like that."

"Wasn't he? How about Wayne Hitchcock, Pete Weston . . . ?"

"Pete Weston!" She spat it out. She struck

him savagely, then clawed. He flung her away and walked across the room. Under anger, under everything, was a maddening feeling that Weston was not the only man in the country who was not too smart. Good Lord, no! It couldn't be that she was making a fool of him for fun.

They dressed in silence. He was at the door when she ran to him, putting her arms around him. "I'm sorry, Brock. Tonight. . . ."

"I'm going to Turret tonight . . . leaving at twelve!"

"What for?" Her curiosity was greedy, grasping.

"To buy the Smuggler Mine."

For just a tick of time she was confused, and then she shoved him into the hall and slammed the heavy door. Brock Sargent was confused all the way down the steps. *I must be,* he thought, *completely in love with Monica Hardin.*

Theobold met him at the lobby doors. "I think Alma sees it our way, Sargent, but it's not going to be easy on her. If there was some way . . . ?" He let it drift away. "Better wipe that cheek off, Sargent."

Standing in the dusky street, Sargent did not know which way to jump. At last he decided Tallman was the man to talk to.

256

Before he knew it, he was over his boots in mud and water on the courthouse lawn. He cursed out loud. Working his way around the back of the building, he stepped into a hole and went to his knees.

Tallman was not in his office or in his quarters next to it. The building was dark. All the heat of dead days and the musty smell of dead dreams seemed to be gathered there.

Neither was the sheriff in The Crusher, or the Desert Cafe. Three times Sargent walked by the cafe, catching glimpses of the strain on Alma's face as she served Doc Cobb and Hadley and a train crew.

Morton was sitting in the darkness at his window. "Seen Tallman?" Sargent asked.

"Not since he put his horse away." Morton caught the urgency in Sargent's tone. "I think I can find him, if it's real important."

"It can wait."

Ozanne was the one that was important, but now Sargent was committed to going after Packard. He would have to go, because, if he did not, Tallman would go alone. He lay down on his bed, with no thought of rest.

"Better get some sleep," Morton said.

"That's a long ride."

"To where?"

"Turret."

"Did Tallman tell you?"

"He mentioned going up there at midnight, yes."

Sargent was dozing when the train whistle came mourning in from the direction of the Emigrants. He was sound asleep when a hand shook him.

"Brock-ee!"

Sargent sprang up and bumped against Benny Paez and felt his silent laughter. "Sometime you could lose your throat, sleeping lak that," Paez said. "But eet ees all right thees time. In thee stable a man was sitting with a large rifle, and he asked of me several questions before he said I could come up."

"All right, Sargent?" Morton called up from below.

"All right! Thanks."

"Do we have lamps, or must I talk to a beeg shadow with" — Paez sniffed — "the smell of perfume from a woman all about him? Now the horse smell here ees good, but. . . ."

"You do all right talking, Benny, dark or light." Sargent lit a lamp.

Paez grinned, and shook hands.

"Your wife?" Sargent asked.

"Good. She ees now at thee Lava Rock . . . thee Lava place on thee corner." Paez sat down and was deadly serious in an instant. "Thees Bledsoe. . . ." He shook his head. "He never came back to Turret, so I could not watch heem."

"He's dead."

"Good. Now what I have done. . . . You killed him, of course?"

"No. Somebody else got him after I turned him loose. He knew nothing of Pat. I was sure."

"He ees dead. Good. Above the ceiling of the marshal's office are two roofs, so the place will not be too hot, too cold. Eet ees a narrow place." Paez measured with his hands. "In thee daytime I was afraid to go there, but at night I did, three nights. By removing with my knife a few shingles, a board which was already rotten. . . . three nights I spend there. During two there was notheeng but thee snoring of a deputy below, thee one who ees supposed to walk down alleys now and then to keep thee drunk ones from being robbed. On thees third night, very late, there came Packard. With great anger he kicked thee sleeping deputy into thee street to do his walking.

And then there came thees man who ees boss of the robbery. He. . . ."

"Who?"

"I do not know. Let me tell what I do know. There came thees man. Packard was angry, saying that thee man had hidden thee gold where none of thee others . . . he meant heemself, of course . . . could find eet. Thee man said there was much hotness about thee gold, and eet must estay where eet was until all thee hotness ees gone. The veesitor cursed you, Brock-ee, saying you were thee most dangerous since you were Patrick's fren, and also, perhaps, a very smart spy sent by thee company. Packard said that was easy, but thee other said no, there had been too many killed already. They argued. You weel remember, please, that their voices were low sometimes, so I did not hear every word. Thees I did hear." Paez's eyes glittered. "You were a fool, Packard, to put Josan onto Volpondo. Volpondo was not even working for Western."

"Josan? Was that Ozanne?"

"O-zan-ee. ¡Sí! That ees thee way eet was said. Where ees that one?"

"I don't know. What else did they say?"

"Thee man said thee sheriff was fooled, but that you were sniffing too close to thee

260

truth. He told Packard to put eet een a lump, if he did not lak waiting. There would bee much waiting before any of thee gold was dug up."

"Dug up?" *The man could have lied to Packard.*

"Yes, he said that. Then Packard said, all right, but that he should know where thee iron box was, in case something happened to thee other. The man laughed, but only een hees mouth, and said thee gold was safe upon thee desert. Packard was angry, but he had to put eet in thee lump. . . ."

"To lump it, Benny?"

"To mak a lump of it, *sí*, because he did not know where thee gold was. Thee veesitor said to wait, to have patience, and then thee two of theem would share thee gold between theem. And then he went away."

"Would you recognize the man's voice?"

Paez pushed out his lips. "I do not know. Thee veesitor was nervous. He walked around much, makin' noise. Sometimes Packard, I theenk, slap thee desk, and sometimes they talked so I could not hear at all. You weel remember there was one roof above, one below, with also thee ceiling. *Ai*, thee place was narrow and very hot."

"You did fine, Benny. This fellow said the gold was in the desert, huh?"

Paez shrugged. "He could lie, of course."

"He did," Sargent said. "I think I'm getting this thing straight."

"*Bueno.* Then where is this Josan . . . Ozanne that we weel keel slowly?"

"I don't know. He won't go far, though, because the gold is still around. We'll find him in time."

Paez began to roll a cigarette, his powerful fingers moving deftly, his eyes steady on Sargent, solemn.

"Did Hanawalt have men watching Packard?"

"Hanawalt? I do not know that one, but there were, for a while, two men who watched Packard. Then there was one. A *muchacha* in Grace's place, a *muchacha* who Packard sees much, got thees last watcher very drunk. That was thee night thee veesitor came."

Sargent said: "I'm glad you are away from there, Benny. You may have settled a lot by not tackling Packard by yourself."

"There was a moment when I would have, but by thee time I got from between thee roofs and into thee cool darkness, I could theenk a leetle. So I went home and would not look at Packard all thee next day. Then, later, I watched heem some more, but he

262

did nothing but go to thee trains, to thee saloons, to Grace's at night, so I came to tell you what I knew."

"Tomorrow morning," Sargent said, "the sheriff and I are going to arrest Packard."

Paez grinned. "We weel do that."

"No. You have to stay here, Benny. You must watch for this Ozanne, who killed Pat."

"Always I watch een one place. Then thee killing, lak that of Bledsoe, ees een another. Eef Ozanne ees gone from thee country. . . ."

"We'll be back tomorrow night," Sargent said.

Paez sighed. "You, Brock-ee, and my wife, you would keep me from being as Benny Paez once was. Now I am old and all I am good for ees to watch for people, and crawl eento narrow places."

Sargent grinned. "You'll be old when you're a hundred, Benny. Come on, I'll take you to a man who can tell you more than me about Ozanne, and this man would like to find Ozanne also."

Paez went down the steps like a great cat, almost silently.

"Morton," Sargent said to the darkness of the stable.

"Here."

Sargent lit a lantern. He introduced Paez and Morton. "Will you see if you can find Benny a little house tomorrow?" Sargent asked. "For him and his wife."

"I can find a dozen. I'll get him the best one."

At The Crusher, Sargent called Weston from the poker game and introduced him at the bar to Paez. "A friend of Sargent's is a friend of mine!" Weston said, and looked around to see if anyone cared to disagree. He squinted at Benny's squat, powerful build. "I'll bet you'd be pretty rough in close, eh, Paez?"

Paez shrugged. His smile was innocent. Weston punched him in the shoulder, and neither the smile nor Paez moved. "We'll get along," Weston said.

Sargent lowered his voice. "Benny, like me, is looking for Ozanne."

"That makes three of us," Weston said. "You know something, Sargent?" His voice was conspiratorial. "There's one thing that will bring Ozanne back here." He gestured with his thumb toward the Lava House. "How about that?"

"Yeah," Sargent said slowly, and he almost added: *You're not dumb, Pete.*

"I'll bet she didn't fool you any," Weston

said. "Dumb as I am, I got onto her a long time ago, about the first day Fletch took me to Triangle."

"You'll give Benny all the help you can, won't you, Pete?"

"Sure! Him and me will get along. One thing she did, Sargent. . . ."

"We got to go right now, Pete, but Benny will be around."

On the street Paez said thoughtfully: "You've had some trouble with thees woman, no, Brock-ee? Who ees thees woman he would talk about?"

"It doesn't matter," Sargent said. "You get word to Bernice you're going to stay here. I'll see you tomorrow night."

"Thees Weston, he ees not thee one," Paez said. "With hees voice below, I would have been blown from between thee two roofs."

Sargent waited in the sheriff's office until eleven thirty. Steps creaked somewhere in the building, and Tallman came down the hall, yawning. He had been in the unfinished furnace room, he said, sleeping where it was cool.

Sargent told him about Paez's spy work. And then, after some hesitation, he told him what Theobold and Alma had seen the night of the robbery.

"I knew she had been there," Tallman said. "I was sitting here at the window. I heard her run up the steps, and later I heard her voice, but I didn't think nothing of it, since the hotel is three blocks from the station."

"Well, is Marty still the main course?"

"Yep!" Tallman said.

As they rode away, Morton's voice came gloomily from the stable. "So long." It reminded Sargent of Tom, the assayer in Turret.

Chapter Nineteen

The bustling roar of the mining camp struck them like a blow. They stopped at the first livery stable at the lower end of the town.

"You won't need an extra horse," Sargent said. "I'm riding the train back tonight."

"I see. I see your point." Tallman looked up the street. "In all that uproar we ought to be able to get our job done quiet-like and be away in no time. Let's ride on up. . . ."

"Let's not," a voice said. Marty Packard stepped from the office of the livery stable, a shotgun in his hands. "Get down right here." He was covering them from the left side. His face read death.

Scared men began to appear from the corrals, from the stable, from the office behind Packard, faces scared and faces dripping expressions of cruel anticipation.

Tallman looked at Sargent and shook his head gently. He knew what Sargent was thinking. During the instant when their feet touched ground. . . . Packard knew it, too. He did not tell them to drop their pistols.

He waited wickedly for them to make their try. The shotgun had two barrels, and they were close.

They stood on the ground, and Packard still waited, hoping. The other faces began to come closer.

"That's the sheriff, Packard!" someone said.

"He's off his range! Keep your mouth shut!" Packard said savagely.

Tallman said quite calmly: "We're dropping our gun belts, Packard."

The gun belts struck the ground.

"Now what's the idea?" Tallman asked. "What's the charge, Packard?"

"This is my town," the marshal said. "I'll decide that later."

Sargent thought: *Tallman's being here caught him by surprise. He expected only me. Who told him?*

"When we go to jail, to give you time to make up a fake charge," Tallman said, "we'll go around the hill, not through the town, so that nothing's going to happen in the crowd to make you claim we tried to escape. You hear that, men?"

The crowd had grown. Someone said: "Yeah, you're right, Sheriff!"

Packard said: "We'll go as I damn' please!" But he did take them around the hill, and even then the crowd that followed grew larger all the time.

The jail was stone, two feet thick, and the back part was built against solid rock. There was a jailer's office in front, a steel door to a bullpen, and four steel-grated cells beyond that. Packard personally put the two prisoners in cells angling corners across the bullpen where drunks were lying on wet concrete. The bolts clicked greasily. Packard lowered his shotgun. On the way across the bullpen a drunk clutched at his legs. Packard kicked him.

The main street door was closed and locked. Someone had tossed the two gun belts inside. One of the jailers, a powerfully built man with a cadaverous face, hung them on pegs behind a stove.

"I'll sell those myself, Fuller," Packard said. "Remember that."

"Sure, Marty. What's the charge on them two?"

"Carrying firearms, disturbing the peace, resisting arrest. Suspicion of armed robbery."

"Dandies!" Fuller laughed.

The second jailer started to write. "What's their names, Marty?"

"Brock Sargent is the hardcase one. I'll have to find out about the old guy. No visitors, Fuller. Understand?"

Packard went out.

"Fuller!" Tallman called. "You know who I am, all right. Sargent's my deputy. You'd better send someone for Joe Millington at the Smuggler."

"You heard the sheriff, too," Sargent said.

Fuller unlocked the outer door. He began to unreel a firehose from the wall, smiling. "We let the drunks mumble . . . some," he said, "but sober people got to be quiet in here."

Tallman said calmly: "They got a reservoir two thousand feet above town, Sargent. I've always heard they used that firehose to smash the guts in men." He said to Fuller in the same quiet voice: "Go back and scratch your lice, you miserable son of a bitch."

The other jailer peered in. "I think that is the sheriff, after all," he said.

Fuller reeled the hose reluctantly. He stepped hard on the belly of a little drunken man on his way.

Tallman sighed. "We ought to be able to smash out of here with our heads. I know *they're* solid enough."

Sargent examined his cell. The back wall was blasted into the mountain. The sides were stone, and the mortar was firm. The steel door was barred with rods an inch in diameter, and there were two bolts on the door.

After a while Sargent sat down on the bunk. The blankets were sodden. He watched a bedbug scuttle into a crack in the masonry. He rose and tried to see across to Tallman's cell, but the angle was too sharp. A drunk in the bullpen rolled over and groaned. Fuller put his feet on his desk. He belched loudly and began to scratch his head with both hands.

There was no way to crack out of the Turret jail, but Sargent kept trying to think of a way. *Packard would not hold them too long, just long enough to think up some way of getting rid of them. He had to get rid of them. But who had sent the word ahead?*

Anyone might have seen them leave Weston. Morton knew. Hanawalt might have guessed. He was a hard man to fool. And still, Sargent was sure that Packard had expected only him — not Tallman, too. If he had come alone, Sargent would be dead now. The fact that Tallman was still sheriff, when Weston alone could not elect him, proved that he was popular up here also — and that had been enough to give Packard a little pause.

Eventually Sargent admitted to himself

that Monica had known, too, but that was all he would admit. He held the bars of his door, watching the men in the bullpen. Some of them were coming out of it, sitting up against the wall, bruised and sick. He could not see Tallman at all.

Packard was up to his neck now, worried and desperate. A smart man might be able to think of a clever way out of this since it included the sheriff, but Packard was not smart. His plan would run to violence. Word would get around town quickly that the sheriff was in jail. Packard would have to come up with something mighty soon. One hundred thousand dollars was at stake.

Sargent stared at the gun belt in the jailer's office. It might as well have been in Wyoming. He wondered what they had done with Windy. He wished he had not quarreled with Monica. Being trapped and helpless hampered a man's thinking.

He went over to the bunk and threw the sodden blankets and mattress on the floor. The bunk was iron, welded by a blacksmith, bolted to the floor. Pete Weston could not have pulled it apart. There was too much space between the iron slats for a man to sit down without a mattress. Sargent flung the blankets and the mattress back on the rusty iron and began to pace the floor.

Packard would do it when he had them alone. He would not trust his deputies in a matter like that.

Fuller laughed when he heard the pacing. "You'll get used to it," he said.

Shortly afterward two deputy marshals came in. One of them said to Fuller: "The J. P. wants a couple of men sober enough to stand up in court. Marty says he'll be over pretty quick for the two cell cases."

There it was. Packard would start somewhere with Sargent and Tallman, and then afterward he would say they had tried to escape.

One of the deputies went away with two men Fuller picked out of the bullpen. The other deputy began to examine Sargent's pistol. "Not bad," he said with greed dripping from his voice.

"Packard will handle those himself," Fuller said.

"Yeah. All we get is the suicide specials and the junk bulldogs." The deputy sat down, tilting his chair against the wall under the pistols. He pulled his hat low.

"I'm tired of you sleeping in here, Lathrop," Fuller growled. "This ain't no hotel."

"I'm tired of you telling me that, too," Lathrop said. "That makes us even, so shut up." He wriggled his back against the wall, put his feet on a wood box, and began to doze.

Sargent heard the voices outside and could not believe what he heard, a protesting voice, a burly, outraged voice. The office doorknob turned. A boot kicked the door wide open. Fuller leaped up, reaching for his gun.

Pete Weston came in. He was holding Benny Paez by the collar. Paez's hair was hanging in his eyes. His face was bloody, and he was moving his hands in feeble protest.

"What the hell?" Fuller asked.

Weston flung Paez forward. "He tried to rob me, right on the street! I smacked him. Packard was busy, so he said to haul him over here."

"Yeah." Fuller put his gun away. "That's the Mex hosteler from Bayhead's livery. We had him here before."

Weston was looking from side to side around the room. Paez leaned on the desk with both hands, shaking his head. The deputy who had been asleep had risen. He started to shut the door. "Hey!" he cried. "That blue roan out there. . . ."

Weston turned around. "Where?"

The deputy reached for his pistol. Weston

knocked him the full length of the room and did not wait to see him light before he leaped at the second jailer. Paez's head snapped up from the desk, and he hit Fuller in the throat, driving him back against the steel door. Paez held him there and hammered him long after Fuller was held up by no more than the pressure of the blows.

Weston reached the second jailer just as the man got his hands on a shotgun. Sargent saw the blow. It seemed to hang a long time in the air, but, when it landed, the jailer went one way and the shotgun another. The man hit the wall with a sodden sound that said: That's all.

Lathrop had not moved after Weston's initial blow stretched him across the wood box. Men in the bullpen began to stagger up.

Weston tried to pull the steel door down with his hands. "Here's about the only thing around here that shows resistance!" he said.

Paez kicked the outside door shut. "Not loudly, Pedro," he said. He took keys from Fuller's desk. "Let no one but thee sheriff and Brock-ee escape."

He unlocked the first door.

Weston swept the drunks toward a corner with both hands outspread. "Easy now!" he said. "This ain't no general break-out, not for a while at least."

Paez grinned as he unlocked Sargent's cell, and then he trotted across the bullpen to release Tallman.

"How do you like this place, Sheriff?" Weston asked. "They throwed me in here once and. . . ."

"Sheriff, huh?" One of the bullpen characters was holding himself up by hanging to the bars. "The lousy law!"

His eyes showed how confused his mind was. He spun away from the bars and struck at Tallman. It was more of a lurch and a pawing movement than a blow, but Tallman was not looking. The impact caught Tallman off-balance. His boots skidded on the wet floor. He fell, grabbing at a cell bar. The door swung out and threw him hard, and he lit on his shoulder. His face was gray when Paez helped him rise. The confused drunk took a swing at Weston then, and fell flat before he could finish the blow.

Sargent had his hands full at the outer door, hurling back men who were wild to escape. Behind him he heard one of the jailers stir and groan.

Then Weston installed bullpen order in a matter of seconds. "And stay here, like I said!" he yelled, but there were some who could no longer hear.

Paez and Sargent dragged the unconscious jailers and the deputy inside and locked them in the open cell, heaped on the floor together, with Fuller on the bottom.

"We ought to turn the firehose on 'em," Weston growled. "That's what they done to me after I got slugged with a bottle in a fight here once."

"I know about thee water, too," Paez said, "but there ees no time. How ees thee shoulder, Sheriff?"

Tallman was still gray-faced, holding his right arm with his left hand. "All right. Let's go."

"Take Windy with you," Sargent said. He buckled on Fuller's gun belt. "I'll bring Packard in on tonight's train."

"Oh, no!" Weston said. "If you stay, we all stay. Me, anyway."

"That would be a sure way to get in a wonderful jam," Sargent said. "Four horses leave here with four riders, only I won't be one of them."

Paez was peering out the door. "All ees clear . . . now."

"I came here for a good scrap . . . ," Weston began.

"What I saw and heard wasn't exactly a quilting bee, Pete." Tallman grinned. "Sargent is right. Four of us will be sure to get caught and cause a shoot-out. I'm going to stay."

"No," Sargent said. "Not with that shoulder." He unlocked the bullpen door and beckoned to a man who looked able to stay in a saddle. "Here's the fourth rider."

"Maybe he ees a horse thief," Paez said. "However, get another one to ride and I will estay."

"I'm the one," Weston said. "I got a grudge."

"I ain't no horse thief," the released man said. "I got into a scrap at the Golden Bear. I'll ride your horse anywhere, as long as it's away from this town."

"Everybody shut up!" Sargent said. "We'll all be back in the can at this rate. Get 'em going, Tallman."

"I don't like it," the sheriff said.

"Neither do I," Sargent said, "but that's the way it's going to stack."

"Where'll you hide out?" Tallman asked. He looked over Paez's shoulder, out the door.

Thinking of the men in the bullpen, Sargent said: "I'll go to the Smuggler Mine. Millington will take care of me, until it's time to make my play."

"I still stay," Weston said.

"Come on, Pete," Tallman walked out casually. "The coast is clear . . . for the moment."

"But . . . !" Weston was not going to leave.

"A great job, Pete," Sargent said. "But what will Fletcher Hitchcock say if you get in real trouble here?"

"I . . . !" Weston scowled. He tipped the desk over and went out.

Paez was the last. "Ah, that Pedro, he ees a good one. At thee bar, we had a few drinks. I said you had gone after thee marshal. He said. . . ."

"How many people heard you?"

"Not one, Brock-ee. You know better."

"I'm glad you came, Benny. Thanks, and beat it!"

Paez shrugged. "Always I run away." He left.

Sargent heard the horses move out slowly. He put the jail keys on the floor, far enough from the steel door so that it would take a long-armed man several stretches to reach them from the bullpen.

From a mine dump above the jail he watched four horses boil out of town. They left considerable interest in their wake but no pursuit. Men began to emerge from the jail, scattering toward town. Packard would have some of them before long.

Sargent hoped the marshal would catch only men who would not cough up everything they knew about his staying, but that was a false hope, he knew. After a leisurely trip past several tunnels, he worked his way down across the West Fork on a footbridge to a back street. There were eight thousand people living here. Very few knew him. Even so, there were too many people on this back street to suit him, and every one of them seemed to eye him with undue interest. He tried not to hurry to where he was going.

Tom, the assayer, side whiskers, derby hat, and cigar, did not glance up from the paper he was writing on when Sargent entered the shop. Sargent went past the counter and toward the back room.

"Just a minute, mister."

Sargent looked around squarely into the round mouth of a horse pistol. Ashes spilled on Tom's vest as he rolled his cigar. "Oh!" he said. "Yeah." He put the gun away and followed Sargent into the back room, closing the door.

"Mike just left."

"When did the light engine get in?"

"A little after two last night."

It was not good. *Jail might be a safer place,* Sargent thought. He said: "I didn't figure he'd be here till this morning."

"He's like a flea, back and forth between here and the desert." Tom chewed his cigar. "Well, cook up, sleep, whatever you want to do. Just don't make no noise when a customer comes into the other room."

The door closed behind the assayer. Tensely Sargent waited for sounds of the front door. Tom cleared his throat and mildly cursed a blob of ink, and then he was quiet. Sargent went over to the back door. Besides the heavy bar, snug in half-inch iron, there was a huge lock on the inside.

He opened the middle door a crack. "Tom, I want to watch the back of the Golden Bear."

"I thought Mike gave up on the girls."

"There's another deal coming up maybe."

"All right. Just a minute." After a while Tom came in and unlocked the padlock.

Tom did not know the full score, or else he knew so much that Sargent was living on borrowed time. If Tom ever left by the front door, he would lose a visitor through the back door. Customers came in steadily. Sargent listened to the talk, standing close to the middle door, with his gun out.

Nothing but assay business went on, but each customer caused a tearing at Sargent's nerves. He cooked ham and eggs and ate them, sitting on a chair near the back door with his ears cocked for sounds from the front. He was eating when a man came in the front, thumped samples on the counter, and began to laugh.

"One finally backed up on Marty Packard," he said. "He throwed two drifters in the can this morning, and somebody got 'em out. You remember that big cowboy from down Weston way . . . the one that was tearing up the Silver Music Hall one night, until somebody crowned him with a quart bottle?"

"No," Tom said. "You want this run for silver, too?"

"Just gold, Tom. Well, this big cowboy was in on the break. He damned nigh killed Fuller and Lathrop, and that Mex who used to work at Bayhead's was in on it, too. They throwed everybody in a cell and high-tailed, after turning the jail out. Packard's been like a shedding rattler. He thinks one of 'em hid out. He's been at the Smuggler Mine for an hour, even prowled through Missus Millington's bedroom. Joe Millington is fit to be tied."

"That's mighty interesting," Tom said. "I'll run this tonight, Bill. Get it in the morning. So long."

Sargent put his gun away when the front door closed and made the little bell tinkle. Five minutes later, Tom came in. The briefest of smiles winked around his cigar.

"No wonder you wanted the back door open." The smile came again. It was a Hanawalt trademark, no doubt about it.

"You and Mike are brothers, huh?" Sargent tried to make it sound more musing than question.

"Yeah?" Tom said absently. "One thing, when you leave, don't figure on the train. Packard will be there. He always watches the trains, going and coming."

Sargent sat in the chair, watching the alley, listening to every sound in the other room. He had never been a jumpy man, but now he was. It made a long day of it. All Tom Hanawalt had to do was write a few words and give the paper to a customer. Marty Packard would not be forced to jail Sargent a second time.

Tom came in and ate a leisurely meal. He invited Sargent to join him, and Sargent drank two cups of coffee, sitting by the door.

"When is the eastbound due?"

"Five oh five. That's a good time to hike the other way, all right. I can send a man for a horse."

At four-thirty Sargent went out the back door. Tom was at the furnace. "So long," he said.

The bar came down behind the door while Sargent was studying the alley. He wanted to run, but he forced himself to walk away slowly. Two drunks were lying against the back wall of a saloon. Sargent dropped his wide-brimmed hat in the lap of one and took the fellow's battered digging hat. The man was not too drunk.

"Not bad," he said, examining Sargent's hat. "Want to trade the rest?"

That helped to steady Sargent. He exchanged jumpers with the man, getting a mud-spattered one that was about the right size. He eyed the fellow's lunch bucket.

"Take it!" the miner said, waving his hand, grinning. "I didn't go to work this morning, and the old lady will use it to beat my skull in when I go home . . . if I ever do."

In the throng of miners on the street, Sargent might have been one of them, except for his boots and pants. The station was the problem. There were too many people waiting to see the train come in. Sargent wandered along the track and talked to a switchman. From the corner of his eye he saw Marty Packard stride across the cinders near the station, threading arrogantly among the waiting people, now and then stopping to question a man. Packard no doubt loved the show he put on here twice a day.

The switchman said: "There she comes. Another day, another dollar, a million days. . . ."

Sargent was walking away, toward where he judged the express car would stop. A Western wagon was backing toward the platform. Farther down the track a Mexican section crew was trudging up, tools on their shoulders.

Joe Gipp was at the throttle of the Mikado as it eased past. Packard waved at him, then walked along the platform, studying the passengers with hard eyes.

Jack Zellers was the messenger. As the express car came to a stop, Sargent lifted his hat long enough for Zellers to see his face clearly. There was recognition.

"Hanawalt's orders," Sargent said. "I want you to call Packard over here in a minute."

Zellers gulped. "He . . . he always comes down here anyway, Sargent."

"He and I are riding in the express car to Weston."

"I can't. . . ."

"Hanawalt's orders."

Zellers nodded. He glanced toward Packard. The marshal was coming slowly along the platform, peering into the coaches as he walked. There was a large pile of express mail in the doorway. Two swampers and a teamster came over from the wagon and began to unload it.

Zellers spoke a few short words. The three men went back to the wagon as if they had touched hot iron. Sargent walked over to them. "Listen, you!" he said softly. "Don't stare at him. Look somewhere else!"

Packard came up. He said, "Hi there, Zellers . . . ," and then his eyes caught Sargent's boots and pants. The glance ran up to Sargent's face before the marshal started his draw.

It was not quite an even break, Sargent thought, *because he had been waiting, knowing what he was going to do. But, if there was advantage in that, he liked it and was glad to take it.*

Packard was fast but not careless. He aimed after drawing. It was only the difference of a shattering second, but Sargent took his chance then. He shot for Packard's gun arm. The marshal's pistol blasted. The bullet sent the section crew diving under freight cars. Packard's right arm swung back as if a fence post had struck it, and his right foot went back to catch him. And almost in the same motion his left hand went under his coat.

The shoulder pistol was almost clear when Sargent's words got through the deadness on Packard's face.

"Hold it, Packard!"

There was a tick of time when both of them might have died, and then Packard chose life and dropped the hide-out pistol. He sat down on the platform and would not rise, and there was cunning and hatred on his face.

"Get in that express car!" Sargent said.

Packard shook his head, glancing toward the crowd surging from the station.

"Get up, or I'll . . . !"

"No you won't, Sargent. You're done."

They wouldn't know the straight of this, that crowd, and Sargent would not have time to explain. He put his gun away and stooped to lift Packard from behind.

The marshal clung to the edge of the platform and yelled for help. Frantically Sargent looked at the expressmen peering over the platform edge. He saw at once he could expect no help there.

One of the section men was coming on the run, a squat man with a knife in his hand. He poised the steel close to Packard's vest. It was Benny Paez. "Your estomach een your lap, *señor?* Or do you weesh to get eento thee car?"

Packard obeyed then. Sargent waved his hands at the crowd. "Get back! It's all over!"

With a loud grunt Pete Weston came over the forward coupling of the express car. "Get back!" he roared. "We're all U. S. marshals!" His face and the gun he waved carelessly gave the curious crowd pause.

Sargent said to Paez, "Run down and tell the engineer to start. Tell him what's up." He hoped Joe Gipp would understand and act.

Paez slid open the door away from the platform and leaped down. It seemed like a very long wait. Someone had carried the news uptown, and now men were running toward the station. The expressmen edged forward. "We got shipments to get," one said.

"Your shipments will come back from Weston tomorrow," Sargent said. He looked at Zellers.

"Hanawalt's orders," Zellers said numbly, watching the pistol Sargent was holding on Marty Packard.

Paez came running back. "Thee engeeneer asked many questions, but maybe he will go." As he spoke, the train began to take up slack.

Weston was still on the platform. "To hell with Turret!" he bellowed. He grabbed a handiron and came thumping into the express car.

"I don't know about this," Zellers said. "It's against regulations."

"We're all Pinkerton men!" Weston said. "Except me. I'm president of the railroad, so forget the regulations." He walked over to Packard, who was sitting on the pile of express boxes. "Lucky for you, you're shot, or I'd demonstrate what I think of the way your deputies beat me that time you had me throwed in jail . . . and about that water they turned on me."

Packard did not hear. He was looking toward something more threatening than big Pete Weston.

"Where's Tallman?" Sargent asked.

"A few miles out of town we left heem. Hees shoulder, she was pretty bad." Paez drew his knife, eyeing Packard.

"Where's your horses?" Sargent asked.

"Thees one you picked from thee jail, he waited weeth thee horses on thee hill above thee depot. When thee train was gone, eef we did not come, he would go to Weston. Now he ees doing that. I hope he ees not a horse thief."

Sargent grinned. "How'd you know I'd be at the station?"

"Where else would one be able to catch Packard away from a beeg crowd?" Paez asked.

Sargent laughed. "You must have been a first-class revolutionist, Benny!"

"*Ai, sí,* I was a good one." Paez pushed out his lips. "But always we lost." He pointed the knife at Packard. "Thees time we win. The great marshal ees not well eenside heem. Shall we find out some theengs about Patrick, no?"

Grayness was on Packard's face. Blood from his arm was spilling from his fingers, but he was not thinking of his wound. He was thinking, with a stark, sick fear, of something else.

"No, Benny," Sargent said.

Packard would spill his guts to try to save his neck. Some men were tough when they were in the right place, but like some plants their toughness could not stand transplanting. Packard would talk. Let him think about it first. Besides, there was Zellers to overhear anything that was said.

The train rolled clear of town. Standing with one door partly open, Weston thumbed his nose at ticket-holders who had made a futile run to board on the fly.

"There goes your town, Packard," Sargent said.

The marshal was talking to himself. "I didn't kill anybody," he muttered.

They began to roll faster, with the flanges squealing on the curves. Weston slid the door shut. He stared at Packard while Sargent was cutting away the man's sleeve to look at the wound.

"Huh! Just scratched," Weston said. He lay down and went to sleep in minutes, snoring like an over-fed bear.

The arm was broken. It was bleeding badly. Sargent did what he could. Doc Cobb could do the rest. Paez trimmed his nails with his knife and kept watching the marshal.

"I don't know about this," Zellers said. "You sure Hanawalt said it was all right to ride . . . ?"

"It's all right," Sargent said. He looked at Packard. "There's one of the wheels in the safe stealing."

"Him!" Zellers gulped.

"Mike Hanawalt ought to be mighty pleased with the way you helped, Zellers, don't you think?"

Paez grinned. "Fine help, *señor!*"

Several expressions crossed Zellers's features, the most lasting a look of relief. The job — the blessed job he loved to curse — was safe. "Yeah, I guess I did help."

"When do we hit the West Fork?" Sargent asked.

Zellers was still looking at Packard. "About an hour. This is only my second trip on the new run since Hitchcock was made acting agent at Weston. About an hour, I think."

Chapter Twenty

Sargent prowled the car. Wired to a stanchion were several narrow boards. He found a greasy spot on the floor and got down to sniff. "What're the slats for, Zellers?"

"Sometimes a shipment needs to be crated a little better. Generally we got quite a pile of boards there."

"You got a hammer and saw too, then? Nails?"

"Sure. Right there under the desk."

"Who spilled the kerosene?"

"From a lamp, I guess. I never paid any attention." Zellers wasn't greatly interested now. "Is there some?"

"Right here."

"I never noticed."

Paez got down and sniffed. "Coal oil." He looked at Sargent and shrugged. "I theenk I weel sleep now. Thees smelling thee floors mak a great weariness."

"Do the shotgun guards always quit the train at Turret, even if something comes up that says they should stay?" Sargent asked.

"You mean like the night of the robbery?"

"Yeah."

"Hanawalt's cousin always unloads wherever the shipment he's supposed to be guarding is consigned, no matter if the shipment does go on."

"Does that happen sometimes?"

"Sure. Four or five times the Smuggler payroll has been taken on through to Weston, sometimes even farther. That's so there won't be any regular pattern. Joe Millington at the Smuggler has always been scared to death he'd lose a payroll right in town . . . after he'd signed for it. Hey! I'm talking a lot to you, and you said you weren't. . . ."

"I'm a deputy sheriff now," Sargent said. "Has that pile of boards varied much . . . at any certain time?"

Zellers shook his head. "I wired those boards there myself, and we haven't had to repair a crated shipment for a month, maybe longer."

"You're sure . . . that the boards haven't been gone all at one time?"

"I know they haven't."

The train rocked on a curve, and Sargent lurched against the side. The pile of express began to shift, and Zellers leaped to stow it inside the stanchions.

Sargent and Paez helped, and, when the job was done, Sargent said: "You say you sometimes have quite a pile of boards there. How many more than . . . ?"

"I meant quite a few, six or seven more than we got there now."

The boards were oak, about four inches wide, not longer than four feet. Sargent eyed them doubtfully, making a quick estimate. Even with six or seven more. . . .

"I gave him the boards," Packard said. He was slumped against the side of the car, staring at nothing. "I shipped them, all wrapped in burlap, crated. I shipped the two sacks of sand, too, as ore."

"What the hell is he talking about?" Zellers asked.

"Out of his head," Sargent said. He knew what Packard was talking about. It filled in everything that had been missing.

"I shipped to a fictitious . . . ," Packard continued.

"Shut up!" Sargent said. "You can do your talking later."

"He don't sound like he was out of his head," Zellers said.

When they came out of the curves on the steep grade and began to follow close to the East Fork, Sargent was standing on the river side, with the door partly opened. He stood there with his eyes narrowed until dusk began to settle; and not long after that they were in Weston.

It was, Sargent thought, like coming home. Not since he had ridden down the hill to the Double S, more than ten years before, had any place been home to him.

His first thought when the train began to slow was: *Maybe Monica would be at the station.* She was not there. Sheriff Tallman was, his arm in a sling, and with him was Doc Cobb and Ulysses Morton.

"I never thought he'd fade like that," Tallman said, watching Packard as Paez and Sargent helped him from the car.

"I want a lawyer," Packard said.

"We got one," Tallman said, "but he's also the judge. I guess your lawyer will have to come from your town, Packard."

"*Ai,* how they are celebrating up there tonight, you bet!" Paez said.

The relief messenger came aboard. *It would be two days before he was back,* Sargent thought. He said to Zellers: "Better come over to the courthouse with us."

"No need for us." Paez glanced toward the Emigrants. "I hope thee *hombre* weeth thee horses does not esteal them. He was from jail, but still" — he grinned wickedly at Tallman and Sargent — "sometimes one finds honest people een thee jail!"

Weston and Paez went toward town, laughing.

"You come over, too, Ulysses," Tallman said. "You been in this thing from the first, and burying most of the customers."

Doc Cobb worked ruthlessly on Packard's arm. He said the break was from a glancing impact, without shattering, and that Packard could be treated in jail. That was where Tallman put the marshal.

"Feel like talking now?" Tallman asked.

Packard had stood up under Cobb's probing and cleaning without wincing. He was safe now. Things were not so bad. "I want Burke Moniyan. I got nothing to say."

"You talked enough on the train," Sargent said. "You said so yourself . . . before witnesses."

A cold fear was growing in Sargent. He had seen it happen before, a blood-guilty man whose guilt became lost in the mazes of the law, concealed by the mesh of a lawyer's shouted words.

Tallman looked at Sargent. "He don't know everything we got. Let him wonder about what we know of the man who talked to him in his office the other night in Turret."

Packard tried to sit up on his bunk. His

eyes slid sidewise toward the cell walls. "I want a lawyer." He was not so confident now.

"A man turns state's evidence. I ain't got no respect for that kind," Tallman mused. "Still, they get off without the rope a lot of times. Come on, Sargent."

They went back to Tallman's office. Cobb had left. Morton and Zellers were still waiting.

"Packard won't talk." Sargent looked at Zellers. "He never said a thing on the train, either. You remember how quiet he was, Zellers?"

After a while Zellers nodded, his Adam's apple moving as he swallowed. "I remember. He didn't say nothing."

"Just keep remembering, Zellers. Maybe Mike Hanawalt will make you an agent in a town where they have a fine poker game every night. He can go now, huh, Sheriff?"

"Sure, sure!" Tallman said. "It would help some if I knew what the hell you were talking about."

They heard Zellers curse when he struck the water in the yard. "I ought to turn that off," Tallman mused. "But Hadley and me are feuding about it. Well, let's hear things."

Sargent told him about taking Packard.

"Who warned Packard in the first place?" he asked.

Morton stirred a little in his chair in the corner. "It occurred to me that someone might warn someone else about you two. I didn't know who you were after, but I guessed it was important. I watched the telegraph office. One local wire went out, as far as I know. A boy took it down. Williams wouldn't say what it was or who sent it."

"I think I know," Sargent said. "We'll get to that later." He told them what he had figured out in the express car on the way down.

"Simple," Tallman said. "So simple that it made the rest of us the same way. Packard furnished the boards and the weight to put in the box, enough weight to make the wagon groan when they dumped it. Zellers probably never even looked, and the rest were too far away. Black paint, cleaned up by the coal oil, eh?"

"It must have been," Sargent said. "Shall we go get him?"

"We could," Tallman said slowly, "but won't he lead us to the money . . . as soon as he knows about Packard?"

"We can find the safe."

"I know," Tallman said, "but it's an awful

piece of ground to search, hole by hole."

"I'm afraid Ozanne is out there now," Sargent said.

"That's where he'd be, all right. That's where we'll go tomorrow." Tallman rubbed his face. "When this is over, I'm gophering up in the furnace room and sleeping for four days, and I'm going to tell every pet rat down there to bite the hell out of anyone who wants to see me."

"We'll let him go until tomorrow, then?"

"Let's try it." A vagueness lay on Tallman's long face, a distaste for the shaping of events. "One man hauled it away from the wagon. One man, although it took several to load it. You see, it had to bounce the wagon when they dumped it at the train. Ozanne went into the desert alone. It was tough to handle, even with the sand gone, when he fouled up on that gully bank. He took it apart piece by piece before he burned it. That's why there wasn't any nails in the ashes." Tallman blinked wearily. "I had another go at Gin Carstairs. You have to drag things out of people around here with a long rope and not too much force. It shapes like this. Brand went over from the chutes that night and helped load it on the rack. Ozanne took off alone with it. He scattered the horses there on the lava. They moved around after that long enough to get their bearings, and then the three riderless ones hit straight back to the camp at the railroad. Whitey Fallon was riding with the rest of us toward the Emigrants. Carstairs was asleep, really asleep then. Brand unsaddled the three horses and put them in the rope corral. But there was that brown lava rock dust on their pasterns. The next morning Carstairs seen it. Brand said the horses had busted away and taken a trip on their own. There's lava just across the river right here, you know. Carstairs let it go . . . not being too important to anyone right then. Finally, when I went by Anchor on the way home today, I got it out of him."

A splashing and a cursing outside told that another man had struck the moat. Mike Hanawalt came in, stamping his boots.

"You got him, eh? Where is he?"

"Asleep," Tallman said. "Dreaming about lawyers and things."

"Where? I want to see him. By God . . . !"

"Rest yourself," Tallman said calmly. "You know Ulysses Morton?"

"Yes, I rented a horse from him yesterday to take a wild goose chase into the Sodas. What did you get out of Packard?" Hanawalt's voice was tense, quick.

"Blood," Tallman said. "How'd you know we had him at all?"

"We cut in on the wire at our camp every two hours. It came down from Turret, but I didn't know till late this afternoon when I got back from the Sodas. What did he say?"

"He said he wanted a lawyer."

"A lawyer? Oh . . . ?" Hanawalt stared at a year-old calendar on the wall. "He'll get Moniyan from Turret. I better go down and wire our legal staff right now."

A poor way to settle things, Sargent thought, *but that was the way Packard's end of it was likely to wind up.*

"While you're there," Tallman said, "wire one of your spies in the telegraph office in Turret and find out who got a wire from someone here yesterday. What time, Morton?"

"The kid ran down at seven o'clock . . . about," Morton said.

Hanawalt went out the back way quickly. He struck the water again. "Damn you, Tallman!" he yelled. He was back in twenty minutes. "The wire went to Packard. It said, 'Suspect left here at midnight for Turret.' It was signed Marley. Who's Marley?"

Sargent tried to figure it out. The man had known that the trap was closing, that

Packard was a weak link, but strong in one way — as an eliminating agent. But how had he known that Sargent was leaving? If he had seen Sargent and Tallman leave, he surely would have indicated *two* men.

"Who's Marley?" Hanawalt asked again impatiently.

Tallman took a deep breath. "He works for you, Hanawalt."

Hanawalt sat down. Suddenly all his impatience and quickness were gone. "Look, boys, we played ring-around-the-rosey with each other in some things. I wanted to watch Packard myself, figuring anyone else in on the deal would ruin things. You fellows clammed up on me about some other things." His quick smile flashed. "You two did a good job. You did everything, in fact, but you never could hide how much you distrusted me. I wouldn't be surprised if there was a strong feeling that I was behind everything. A man has to take that. I'm used to it. Old Pegram trusted me. That was enough. Now I think we ought to be honest with each other. I'm still sorry I shot Brand, quite aside from the fact that he could have helped clear things up sooner."

Sargent and Tallman looked at each other, and they were in agreement. Morton sat like a gray ghost in his corner. He had been dragged into the affair from the first. He had never wanted any part of it.

"Tell Hanawalt everything, Sargent," Tallman said.

Hanawalt could not sit still during the telling. "I suspected it! That's why I set him in here, where he would be easier to watch, and then I quit suspecting him. I thought maybe that girl . . . Burent's daughter . . . had pushed him into it, the both of them." Hanawalt shook his head. "But after one casual talk with her, I knew better. There's a real woman, gentlemen. I hate to think what this will do to her. What do you suppose got into Burent all at once?"

The flesh of Tallman's face was drooping. "Not all at once, Hanawalt. Years of being here, watching the town die, just taking charity on a job because the Western owner and him was once partners."

"He gambled?" Hanawalt asked. He liked his reasons sharp, simple.

"Just that once," Morton said. "You don't have to need money to want it."

Hanawalt did not examine the remark. He started toward the door. "I'll have my men off the desert, ready to go at daylight. I'll have a wrecker spotted at Mill Siding." He jerked his thumb toward town. "You'll take care of him?"

Tallman nodded. "Watch the water," he said as Hanawalt trotted away.

"Lord, yes! Thanks!"

"Well," Sargent said after some time, "shall we sort of watch him during the night? The train crew . . . probably Zellers, too . . . will talk about Packard."

Tallman rose, standing at the window with one foot on the sill. "I don't want to," he said. "I don't want to. I know him like a book, since he was a kid. There wasn't a better one till that woman. . . . He'll run for the safe, now, I suppose. I know he never wanted a soul killed in this, but still he caused the death of several. He can't get it out of there alone. Maybe he'll leave the country." Tallman was talking to himself. "No, he won't run. I know him. He'll either come to me, or he'll go to his father now. I ain't going after him, and to hell with what the law says. A lawman should never see a kid grow up, or be friends with people, or try to understand what makes them do some things. Maybe a lawman ought to be just like Packard. *My town . . . !* Ozanne is the one. He's the one that started all the killing, him and Marty Packard." Tallman stood silently at the window.

"Let's go to bed, Sargent," Morton said.

They were leaving when a man splashed across the yard, not bothering to curse the water. "Brock-ee!"

It was one of the few times Sargent had ever seen Benny ready to shout and wave his arms. "Easy now, Benny."

"I am een thee Lava House with Bernice. The leetle house, she ees not cleaned good enough to suit her yet. I am asleep . . . almost. The railroaders come, with loud talking about Packard. Soon an *hombre* walks down thee hall from not far. There ees no carpet. He ees gone before my poor brain tells me why eet ees wondering so hard. Thee walk, Brock-ee, thee walk!" Paez tapped his feet against the hall floor. "Thee walk of thee *hombre* who talked to Packard when I was een thee narrow place! I dress quickly, but I have wondered too much first . . . and by then he ees gone."

"And so is one of my horses, I'll bet," Morton said. "Well, he never mistreated a horse."

Paez stepped toward Morton. "You know thees *hombre?*"

"We all know him, Benny," Sargent said. Morton's remark about horses had been small, but it went deep, and it was not going to make things any easier.

"Tomorrow, Paez," Tallman said. "Tomorrow." He went down the hall to look at Packard.

The sheriff's light was out before the three men, making a circle to avoid the flooded yard, reached the street. There was a light in Alma Burent's house. The whole dirty affair had slashed in many directions, Sargent knew, but he could not get out of it now. He was a deputy sheriff, just a badge inside his shirt pocket, and a few words from Sheriff Tallman, but Brock Sargent had never looked lightly on responsibility. And there was still Ozanne.

They passed the Burent house. Sargent looked at the second story of the Lava House. The new lumber of the fire escape made a light streak in the gloom. There was no light in Monica's suite, and Sargent was taken with an uneasy fear he did not want to examine closely.

"Do you know anything about peach trees, Benny?" he asked.

Sargent heard Morton's quick intake of breath.

"*¡Seguro!*" Paez said. "From them comes peaches, and then thee brandy drink that sticks to your fingers badly and makes you first wild and then very seeck."

"He can raise a carrot four feet long, Morton," Sargent said. "Don't let the talk fool you. Do you suppose, if we tied into your orchard proposition, Benny could be the first man to have an orchard?"

"I would like that," Morton said softly. "Your friend, Pat Volpondo, would like it even more."

Paez spoke in Spanish, all his levity gone. "*Sí*, Brock-ee, I think Patrick is smiling somewhere now. Maybe it is the first thing we have said that he likes."

Chapter Twenty-One

The wrecker, its red boom cabled fast, pointing toward the Emigrants, sat on the siding with its crew lying in the shade beneath it. Sargent scrambled up the bank and crossed the tracks. He was carrying a long iron brace rod from one of Morton's freight wagons.

"Who's ahead of me?" he asked.

The wrecker boss was munching a bacon sandwich. He tried to talk and finish his bite at the same time. A strip of bacon did not shear, pulling out in one piece from between the bread. He pulled it in as a horse takes hay. "Just two." He swallowed. "Two old guys, one with a big white mustache."

Hadley? He had been playing poker during the conference in Tallman's office the night before. "A little man with egg on his mustache?"

"Naw. Big, fierce-looking old cuss. Lean. On a horse."

Fletcher Hitchcock. Morton was the other. He had been awake last night when Barrett, the jail escapee, had brought in

Windy and the other two horses. Morton had given his bed to Barrett, saying that he would sleep on the hay at the back end of the stable, but he must have gone to Triangle, for he was not around when Sargent got up. Telling Fletcher Hitchcock must not have been an easy job, in spite of what old Fletch had tried to make the world accept.

"Thanks." Sargent leaned on the iron rod, looking at the wrecker. "Can you make a long pick with that rig?"

"Quite a pick . . . if we have to."

"You're going to have to."

Sargent went up the track, toward where he remembered the roughest part of the cañon to be. Let Hanawalt's boys do the inch-by-inch probing of the river holes. He would try some more spot work.

The West Fork was at low fall run, but the holes down there were deeply worn into the rock bottom. The water made booming sounds. Fifty feet above him Sargent saw the railroad grade. The cañon was tortuous, studded with rocks as large as small houses. Sometimes Sargent waded chest-deep with his gun belt around his shoulders.

The river was dirty yellow from the waste of Turret's mills, but in the shallow places he could see the bottom. He sounded the pools with the rod, poking, feeling, waiting for the jar and sound of metal on metal. Even now he had no real interest in the safe, but the work carried some of the age-old thrill of hunting hidden treasure and the satisfaction of outwitting the other man. But, mainly, he was sure this would lead him to the man who had killed Volpondo.

Below the swirl of a deep pool under a waterfall his rod brought back the right sound and feeling. He tapped again with his hands and wrists submerged. Down there was metal, heavy, thick metal. He looked up at the straight line which marked the railroad embankment.

This could be the right place. The train had met dusk about here last night. On that other night, the brakemen would have been resting in the caboose with the heavy grade behind them. Firemen and engineers look ahead, not back. Rolling out the safe on pipes would have required only seconds up there where the track almost hung over the cañon. Yes, right there at the end of the rod might lie a hundred and nine thousand dollars in gold coin.

Sargent went back to shore and studied the pockets of sand between the rocks. There were no tracks here but his own. The other side of the cañon wall was broken, partly masked by spruce trees. Ozanne probably was working from that side. Sargent might be first here, but he doubted it.

For a while he stared at the pool, and then he left his rod and gun belt on the shore and waded out again. He was under water before he remembered his hat. The river took it.

It seemed a long way down. The rocks were slippery against his fingers, and the cold compressed its force against him. He was ready to give up and go to the surface for air when his left hand touched smooth metal. He held to it, ran his right hand around it. A boxcar wheel!

He sat on a rock afterward, shivering, wiping a fine, greasy film of mill waste from his face. The next time he would size things up more carefully with the rod before he went down. Once more he picked up the long piece of iron and his gun belt and began to work upstream.

The bank on his left became less steep, more broken with slanting cuts, choked with trees and brush. Chest-deep against the current at the foot of a long pool, he was inching ahead to go around a sharp bend when he saw the wet streaks on a rock ahead, a rock too high above the water to have been slashed by the river.

He tried to back up slowly, without noise,

angling toward a huge gray rock near the shore. He slipped, threw out his arm for balance, and made a loud splashing sound. He was clear off-balance when he heard sand crunch on a rock. Someone said in a low, tense voice: "Get him, Chuck!"

There was no time to look or to wonder. Sargent lunged desperately toward shore, holding his pistol high. The narrow cañon thundered with the blast of another pistol as Sargent flung himself the last few feet. The hard *splutt* sent a jet of water above his legs, and then he was clear, rolling to the protection of a rock.

Around the bend sand crunched again. *Two of them,* Sargent thought. *Ozanne and Wayne Hitchcock.* Sargent had been making too much noise of his own, too busy floundering ashore, to be sure about the voices. He looked behind him. There was cover, plenty of it. He should retreat before one man climbed the bank to catch him from above, or crossed the river and worked down through the trees.

That was common sense, and Sargent did not like wild chances. But he thought of Pat Volpondo; and he could not forget that just around the bend was the end of the long trail. A man did what he thought he must do.

He could climb this rock, going over it in a rush, or take snap shots from the top. Neither action held any value. The first would get him killed quickly; the second was a poor compromise. He started up the rock, not having to fake the sounds he wanted to make. Then, bracing his feet solidly, he held his pistol high and leaped as far into the river as he could.

The two shots were touched off by motion. They were not where the motion was, but where it had been expected. For a moment Sargent thought there was no bottom. Water showered up, obscuring his vision, sheering close to the thread of time that marks the line between life and death. He staggered when his feet struck bottom. But he had seen enough: Ozanne and Monica.

Ozanne was standing between two rocks. His smoking pistol was still pointed above the boulder from which Sargent had leaped. The pistol jerked toward Sargent.

A half second is enough for the one that counts, if the shooter does not hurry. Sargent could not afford to hurry now. He saw the brutal impact of his lead, and he knew by the down-tilting muzzle of Ozanne's pistol that one shot had been enough. Past Ozanne's sagging eyes and shock-opened mouth, over his shoulder, Sargent saw Monica's face when she turned from glancing up the wall.

She came in from Ozanne's side. She jarred against Ozanne with both hands, crying: "Get him, Brock!"

She nearly fell when Ozanne offered no resistance, crumpling at her touch. She recovered quickly, staring just a moment at Ozanne, and then she ran to grab Sargent's arm and help him from the river.

"Oh, Brock, Brock! It's been a nightmare ever since he forced me to go with him." She threw her arms around Sargent. He looked over her shoulder, down at Ozanne, who was lying on his side with his eyelids blinking slowly.

Sargent set Monica aside and got down on his knees. "Ozanne, you killed Volpondo, didn't you? Packard told you about him." There was scarcely doubt, but Sargent asked.

Ozanne's lips moved slowly. "You find out."

"He did! He told me so," Monica said.

He looked at her. "You recognized me when I first waded around the rock."

"No!" Monica said.

The dying man made a faint nod. With his last expression Ozanne sent out hatred at Sargent, with his last breath he tried to curse, and then he was nothing but a huddled shape that had been a man, lying with his cheek pressed against a pool of sand between the rocks.

"Brock . . . !"

Without looking at her, Sargent pushed Monica aside when he rose, still looking at Ozanne. This was his vengeance, already shrinking to nothing. The voice of the river was no lighter; the sunshine reaching down was just the same. Pat Volpondo could not know, and Sargent felt no different now, only a little bitter, completely tired.

It was done, and, if it had left an unclean taste, some of that was coming from another source. "You saw me when I first waded around that bend."

"No, Brock! I didn't see you!"

Sargent walked past Monica. At the edge of the water, with rust already gnawing at it, with two ropes around it, lay the safe. The ropes ran back to a Spanish windlass, a simple rig of two poles, one to stand upright and travel in the loop of the ropes, the longer one to twist around the first in little, powerful bites. A man could move much with one of those. He could pull a bugged steer apart with one hand.

"You helped a little?" Sargent asked.

"He made me do it. Brock, you don't think . . . ?"

"Save it for the next idiot, Monica."

"I tried to help you! I pushed him when I saw it was you! I didn't realize he was already shot!"

"That last, I think, is true," Sargent said. He glanced up at the railroad embankment. Fletcher Hitchcock and Morton were looking down. They had been there right after the first shot, Sargent was sure. They certainly had been standing there when he saw Monica's face over Ozanne's shoulder. She had seen them then — and had made her play, and the margin had been so close that Hitchcock and Morton might even now be thinking that she had tried to help Sargent.

He brought his eyes down and looked at her. She was as beautiful as ever. Only time would ever steal that from her.

With fury throwing sparks in her voice, she said: "You're a damned fool, Brock! We could have had this to ourselves if you had told me everything from the first!"

"You heard me and Theobold talking at the desk that day. You ran to Ozanne and told him, and then you tried Wayne Hitchcock. We found out this morning from a kid that he was the one who warned Packard about us."

It was true. She admitted it without saying a word. Only a fine point bothered her. "I didn't have to run to Ozanne," she said. "He came to me. He's been coming to me every night . . . when you weren't in the way."

It hurt, but it did not crush. *At about fifteen you learn a little,* Sargent thought, *and then you learn some more at twenty-eight — or later.* It was late enough for Brock Sargent.

Monica smiled. "He made me go with him. He threatened to kill me. He was crazy jealous. He even forced me to help him with the safe. Of course, I intended to turn him in at the first chance." She mocked Sargent with her smile.

Get him, Chuck! Her story would be believed or, at least, accepted.

"Where's your horses?" he asked.

She pointed to the east side of the cañon. "I think I'll go up on this side, though," she said.

"Sure. Start your campaign early."

"Thank you so much, Mister Sargent. Alma always calls you Mister Sargent, doesn't she?" Monica laughed. She took his arm, and the pressure of her fingers was like the touch of something that crawls out of the night when a man is sleeping on the ground. She felt the difference in him, and laughed again. "I saved your life, Brock, remember?"

She looked at the safe.

He looked at Ozanne.

"There being no survivors of the original discovery, I suppose it could be said that I found the gold, and am entitled to the reward, wouldn't you say, Brock . . . Mister Sargent?"

Someone shouted on the embankment. Two men had joined Hitchcock and Morton — McClellan and another Western special agent. They were pointing across the cañon. Over there a man was climbing up through the trees, a tall man who moved on stiff legs, pulling himself by holding to branches and bushes. He did not seek cover or try to hurry. Wayne Hitchcock must have been quite close, hearing everything, watching, waiting — and now it was all over.

"That's him!" McClellan shouted. His splinted fingers made a white splash against his coat as he raised a rifle. Wayne Hitchcock stopped. He turned, waiting.

His father tore the rifle away from McClellan and tossed it into the cañon. The second agent leaped back, out of Sargent's view. Fletcher Hitchcock drew his pistol. He did not seem to be saying anything, just standing there, shaking his head.

Across the cañon his son went on up, climbing out of sight. Sargent stared at Monica, and she knew what he was thinking.

"Why don't you say I'm responsible for that miserable cripple?" she said. "He was always odd, and he went completely sour after his legs were smashed in that robbery on Costilla Pass."

Wayne Hitchcock had gone sour at Triangle long before that. Sargent knew now how it must have been. "God help you, Monica," he said.

A horse showed for a moment on the east rim, and then Wayne Hitchcock was gone. His father put his pistol away. McClellan began to curse. Monica's clear laugh floated up. "You and Theobold ought to hold revival services, Sargent!"

Chapter Twenty-Two

Fletcher Hitchcock and Whitey Fallon sat in the shade of their horses beside the railroad. Except for their quietness, they might have been another two of the spectators who had swarmed out to see the safe recovered. The wrecker was there, and cable was snaking over the cañon rim.

Benny Paez and Pete Weston, laughing, were trying to direct all operations. McClellan was sitting on a rock, now and then glancing coldly at the Triangle owner. Monica was talking to the other special agent.

Theobold and Morton came across the rails to where Sargent was standing near Fletcher Hitchcock.

It might have been an ordinary day, the way Theobold spoke to Hitchcock. "Sargent and I are going in with Morton on the irrigation thing, Fletch," he said. "I'll turn that land on the East Fork loose to you any time."

Hitchcock nodded gravely. "All right, Tracy. It will be next year before I can do much paying. I'm all tied up with Tug Marshall now."

"We can work it out," Theobold said.

Fallon made little marks with his fingers in the sun-warmed cinders between his legs.

A shout came up from the cañon. Hadley was standing high on a rock, peering down, and now he relayed the news importantly. "It's the gold, Hanawalt says! He just opened her up! He says the gold is there, all right!"

Hitchcock had been waiting to be sure. His face did not change when he stood up. Fallon's face was a savage, blistered mask as he stared at Monica.

"He made a box on the train," Hitchcock said. "He dumped the safe out here. The rest was a fake." He nodded. "See if Hanawalt is coming up, Whitey."

Sheriff Tallman and Mike Hanawalt climbed out of the cañon a few minutes later. Monica went rapidly toward the express official, but Tallman edged her away. Hanawalt was joined by two of his agents as he strode across the rails to Hitchcock.

"All right, Hitchcock, you wanted to be double sure about it . . . it's down there. And now, let's hear your end of it."

"Don't shove on the reins, Hanawalt," Sargent said.

Fallon nodded faintly. He had never been more dangerous, Sargent knew.

"I'll bring him in," Hitchcock said. "I know where he is. He's at Triangle right now, standing by his mother's grave. He came up several days ago to see me. We made up, but he said he couldn't come back. I know why, now."

Hadley jumped from his rock and started to run over to hear the conversation. Holding Monica's arm, Tallman reached out and caught Hadley by the collar and jerked him back. "Private," he said, and nodded toward the cañon. "Go over there and run things."

"What if he doesn't want to come in?" Hanawalt asked. He looked at his two men.

"I said I would go get him." Hitchcock reached for his reins.

"Maybe I'd better send a couple of men to. . . ."

Hitchcock turned. His patience was underlaid with savageness, ready to explode. "I said I would bring him in, Hanawalt. I think you heard."

Monica got away from Tallman then. She came over and touched Hanawalt's arm.

"Come on, Whitey," Hitchcock said.

Fallon would never be closer to refusing to obey a Triangle order than he was at the moment. After Hitchcock had given Monica a long look and ridden away, Fallon still stood beside his horse, staring at nothing. "I learned that boy to ride," he muttered.

He saw the others watching, and then he became bitter and defensive. Pete Weston lumbered across the rails, sheering close to Monica, bumping between Hanawalt's agents.

"Anybody giving Fletch trouble, Whitey?"

"No, Pete." Fallon looked at Monica. He shook his head, and then he swung up and rode after Fletcher Hitchcock.

Monica had seen everything, but her bright run of talk to Hanawalt went on: ". . . and when he told me he had killed a man named Bledsoe, besides this other one that Packard said was a Western agent, Mister Hanawalt, I was so shocked and scared I hardly knew what to do!"

"I imagine, Miss Hardin," Hanawalt said.

"What's your first name?"

"Mike." An odd smile played around Hanawalt's thin lips.

Weston uttered a short, bitter word. Hanawalt looked at him, as if intending to call him for it, and then he looked twice and let it go. The special agents looked away from Weston. He shrugged and went back across the tracks to Paez. Morton, Theobold, and Tallman walked away.

"He said that it was Wayne's idea, Mike, but that he was making certain improvements, so that there would be no one but him left in the end. I was so frightened."

"He thought perhaps the two of you could go away together, I suppose?" Hanawalt asked.

"Yes, that's what he said. Imagine! After forcing me at gunpoint to accompany him." Monica's eyes widened. "I just thought . . . there must be a reward for finding the safe, isn't there?"

"Why, yes." Hanawalt smiled.

Before he walked away to join his friends, Sargent took a long, careful look at Monica Hardin. She was as pretty as that sorrel filly, gleaming in the sun at Trinchera long ago, but she had moved.

The wrecking crew was making the pickup. Strain was on the cable. A man standing on the cañon rim was signaling with a gloved hand. Hadley was giving loud advice.

"I talked some to Fletch early this morning," Morton said. "He thought maybe Wayne would try to clear Burent, claim he was forced to. . . ."

Theobold said: "Alma knows better. Now that it's broken loose, she doesn't want anything hidden. Burent was guilty. Either

Brand or Ozanne killed him as soon as his part was done. Maybe that rap Wayne Hitchcock got was not for show, either. Maybe they tried. . . ."

"Let's see if we can forget it," Sargent said.

Paez came over. "Soch a beeg weight of gold! *Ai,* Brock-ee, eef I had that!"

Sargent smiled. *In time smiling would come a little easier,* he thought. "If you had it, you could finance a revolution, Benny."

"Some fought for gold," Paez said, "and some of us weeth no shoes fought for thees." He picked up a handful of dirt and let it run through his fingers. "And now we weel build thee dam and thee beeg ditch?" He looked into the cañon. "Down there!"

Morton laughed. "No! I'll show you where this afternoon."

"We'll build everything." Sargent saw the rows of peach trees on the hill above Volpondo's grave, and he thought that someday he would stand in Weston and point up there and tell Alma Burent that she had been right all the time.

That would be a start.

About the Author

Steve Frazee was born in Salida, Colorado, and in the decade 1926-1936 he worked in heavy construction and mining in his native state. He also managed to pay his way through Western State College in Gunnison, Colorado, from which in 1937 he graduated with a bachelor's degree in journalism. The same year he also married. He began making major contributions to the Western pulp magazines with stories set in the American West as well as a number of North-Western tales published in *Adventure*. Few can match his Western novels which are notable for their evocative, lyrical descriptions of the open range and the awesome power of natural forces and their effects on human efforts. CRY COYOTE (1955) is memorable for its strong female protagonists who actually influence most of the major events and bring about the resolution of the central conflict in this story of wheat growers and expansionist cattlemen. HIGH CAGE (1957) concerns five miners and a woman snowbound at an isolated gold mine on top of

Bulmer Peak in which the twin themes of the lust for gold and the struggle against the savagery of both the elements and human nature interplay with increasing, almost tormented intensity. BRAGG'S FANCY WOMAN (1966) concerns a free-spirited woman who is able to tame a family of thieves. RENDEZVOUS (1958) ranks as one of the finest mountain man books, and THE WAY THROUGH THE MOUNTAINS (1972) is a major historical novel. Not surprisingly, many of Frazee's novels have become major motion pictures. According to the second edition of TWENTIETH CENTURY WESTERN WRITERS (1991), a Frazee story is possessed of "flawless characterization, particularly when it involves the clash of human passions; believable dialogue; and the ability to create and sustain damp-palmed suspense."